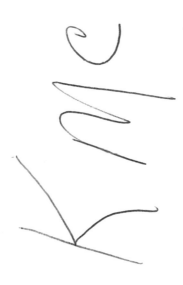

MALICE AFORETHOUGHT

A Selection of Recent Titles by J M Gregson from Severn House

Lambert and Hook Mysteries

GIRL GONE MISSING
TO KILL A WIFE

Detective Inspector Peach Mysteries

MISSING, PRESUMED DEAD
WHO SAW HIM DIE?

8/∞

MALICE AFORETHOUGHT

J. M. Gregson

This first world edition published in Great Britain 1999 by
SEVERN HOUSE PUBLISHERS LTD of
9–15 High Street, Sutton, Surrey SM1 1DF.
This title first published in the U.S.A. 1999 by
SEVERN HOUSE PUBLISHERS INC of
595 Madison Avenue, New York, N.Y. 10022.

British Library Cataloguing in Publication Data

Gregson,   J. M.   (James Michael)
          Malice aforethought
          1.   Lambert,   Superintendent (Fictitious character) - Fiction
          2.   Hook,   Sergeant (Fictitious character) - Fiction
          3.   Police - England - Fiction
          4.   Detective and mystery stories
          I.   Title
          823.9'14 [F]

          ISBN 0-7278-5454-2

Typeset by Hewer Text Ltd
Edinburgh, Scotland.
Printed and bound in Great Britain by
MPG Books Ltd, Bodmin, Cornwall.

One

I t was thoughtful of them to bring back an old man
for this morning's service. The Reverend Tom Dodds
allowed them that. He was totally out of sympathy with
the happy-clappy gatherings which passed for services in
the old church nowadays, but at least they had remembered him for this. He had begun to think that he had
been completely forgotten.

And this year the eleventh of November fell satisfy-
ingly on a Sunday. They would be able to stand through
the two minutes' silence without the hum of traffic and
the blare of horns from the centre of the old town. His
words within the church went well, he thought. He
savoured the cadences as he intoned those sonorous
phrases: the eleventh hour of the eleventh day of the
eleventh month. You could hardly fail with such an
opening. And he did not fail; studying the white, uplifted
faces before him, he could see that he was holding their
attention.

He told them how he had gone into the village school
to talk about the war and found children who had
thought that Desert Rat was a term of abuse, not a
proud label. That was understandable, for that war was

1

almost as far away from today's children as the Crimean War had been for him as a boy. He found it less easy to forgive the forty-year-old mother of two who thought that Rommel was an old film star and had heard of Montgomery only as a golfer. He got little titters of appreciation and approval from his congregation: people were more prepared to be amused in church than when he had first spoken here half a century ago.

There were none there now to preserve the memory of that senseless bloodbath of 1914–18. Old Sam Burgess, who had gone through the Somme at eighteen and had brought his two sticks and his sightless eyes to support the Reverend Dodds for so many years, had died in 1994. And Tom, looking from the lectern to the thinly peopled benches in the cold church, knew that before too long there would be no men there who had fought in the 1939–45 war, which still seemed so vivid to him.

Well, at least his successor, with his open-necked shirts and his resolute social awareness, had thought to bring back an active service padre for this morning's solemn moments of remembrance. Leading the procession out into the mist and cold of the Cotswold morning, Tom Dodds, MC, forgot his seventy-eight years and his dodgy hip and marched as proud and erect as he had on those bright early morning church parades before Alamein and Tobruk, when you could feel the mixture of resolution and fear in every breath of desert air. Not many people knew nowadays how to march with pride, but he would show them how. He owed it to the brave lads and true who had not survived, who had died so that those unthinking, ignorant lads, who revved

2

their motor-bikes now in the car park of the Red Lion, might be free.

Well, you had to look forward, they said, and it was true enough; you couldn't live in the past. All the same, there were some things that should be remembered. And some deaths: the Reverend Tom Dodds marched with stiff dignity to the church gate and the war memorial with its wreaths of blood-red poppies. He said the prayers of thanksgiving for civilisation's survival with closed eyes, as fervently as he had mouthed them when a whole nation had rejoiced over the extinction of the tyrant Hitler in the forties, when the price in blood and death was still fresh in everyone's mind. He finished with those ringing lines: ·

"They shall not grow old, as we that are left grow
  old:
Age shall not weary them, nor the years condemn.
At the going down of the sun and in the morning
We will remember them."

There was a sporadic mutter of "Amens" from his chilled audience at the end of the verse, as there had been with his earlier prayers. Then the circle of people relaxed and began to melt away. Most of them looked relieved that it was over, that a duty had been done. But a few came up and thanked him for the dignity and sincerity of his service, and that made it worthwhile. They were middle-aged and elderly people who had lost relatives in the wars, people for whom the dancing black-and-white images on their television screens were living history, not an incomplete documentary of events long dead.

When they had gone, old Tom Dodds went back into the church that had once been his church, the church which had stood here almost unchanged through five centuries, and thought of the laughing faces he could still remember from the desert days, of the terror of defeat and the exultation of victory which he could still conjure up at will. Those were the days when he had been most alive, when his youth and that of those around him thrilled to the single great task ahead. And soon now, very soon, his own time must come to join those lads from the yesterday which others found so long ago. In that quiet place, with its high stone pillars and its roof built to vault towards the simpler heaven of an earlier age, he thought of his death without rancour. He would wait for his time, as all good Christians must, but he hoped in that moment that it would not be too long before he was called.

He left the church with reluctance, re-entering a world outside with which he rarely felt in harmony. It was cold still, despite the appearance now of a pale sun. The chill had entered his very bones while he thought of times past; he must have sat in the empty church for longer than he realised. He stamped his feet and flapped his thin arms, hearing them crack, willing a reluctant circulation to course some warmth into his aged limbs.

He decided to walk once more round the familiar churchyard that had once been his domain. You never knew now which time would be the last. The angina was getting worse, and his next appearance here might be as the central figure in a funeral cortège; his plot had been reserved for forty years and more now. He looked at it briefly, a thin line of turf between the mounds which covered other former vicars of the parish; it seemed scarcely big enough to accommodate this latest entry. There would be room enough, he knew. And perhaps he would be the last incumbent so interred, for soon everyone would be cremated. It was the modern way, and for a crowded, disease-conscious planet it was no doubt the best way. But he would quite like to be the last of the old interments.

He walked on, past the gargoyles which leered at him as knowingly as ever from the cornices of the ancient stone, down to the humbler parts of the graveyard, where the town and village labourers of bygone eras had been in their narrow cells for ever laid. Old Tom Dodds had learned Gray's *Elegy* by heart seventy years ago in his village school and its phrases came back to him whether he wished them to or not.

He had to admit that the churchyard was better kept now than in his day. A man cut the grass with a hover mower every week, and the worst of the litter which blew in from an uncaring public was removed by a rota of volunteers every two days. Only beneath the high oaks at the far end of the churchyard, where the grass grew longer and the wild daffodils and bluebells flowered in spring, was there the cheerful neglect of his day. The Reverend Dodds found himself moving automatically to that area which had not changed. By the time he regretted the move it was too late for him to avoid its consequences.

The body lay against the old stone wall which marked the boundary of the church's ground. The man's grey eyes stared unseeingly at the steeple of the church and the low clouds beyond it. The thick crust of blood around the throat was almost black. The Reverend Dodds knew a dead man when he saw one, but he knew also the procedures for checking death. He felt gingerly for a carotid artery, registering as he had known he would the absence of any pulse. Then he turned and hurried as fast as his creaking limbs would carry him back towards that modern world he found so alien.

His hip was hurting suddenly, and the hunched shuffling he had cast off for the Remembrance Service was back with him. But the dead, his reason told him, were never in a hurry.

Two

B y one o'clock the gloomy day was improving, as if the heavens recognised that due attention had now been given to the business of Remembrance. The sun was stronger, throwing clear shadows for the first time in the day, removing with its presence all traces of the thin drizzle which had dampened the earlier stages of that Sunday. There were even a few patches of blue sky over the distant Malverns.

Detective Sergeant Bert Hook noticed none of these improvements. For he was playing golf. And not just golf: as a new member of the Oldford Golf Club, he was playing in his first Monthly Medal Competition. Every stroke would be recorded on the card in his companion's back pocket; every stroke would be accumulated, until the results were displayed for all to see on the clubhouse notice board. For honest Bert Hook, who had found as a young man that most sports came easily to him, that was a terrible prospect.

For golf had not come easily to Bert; it had come, indeed, exceeding hard. He had been a cricketer of distinction, a fearsome fast bowler whose fame spread beyond the confines of his native Herefordshire. Secretly, he had believed that any sport where you approached a dead ball in your own time must be easy: golf had cruelly shattered that illusion. Hook had been enticed into this ridiculous, infuriating sport by Superintendent John Lambert, and at this moment he blamed his superior officer for the full range of suffering the stupid game had brought to him. Amongst the greatest of these, he decided, was playing alongside this same bloody John Lambert, with his years of experience in the game, his steady competence, his encouragement to those new to golf, his infuriating calm.

Yes, above all, his infuriating calm. When you were itching to throw your clubs into the pond by the twelfth and yourself after them, the last thing you wanted was a man with his ball on the green and a broad smile as you approached yours in the bunker. "Head down and swing steady," said John Lambert cheerfully. "You can still break a hundred for the round if you keep your head."

"I thought you couldn't advise me in a strokeplay competition," said Hook testily. "In any case, I'd rather you kept your bloody mouth shut."

Any observer would have found it hard to believe that this warring duo enjoyed the most harmonious of working relationships. Within the workings of Oldford CID, Hook deferred to no one in his admiration of Detective Superintendent John Lambert. Woe betide the junior officer who offered the ritual rumblings of derision about high-ranking passengers if Bert Hook was around. Superintendent Lambert was considered a dinosaur among policemen by the new men of the detective force and even by some of his contemporaries, because of his refusal to sit behind a desk and organise the hunt from there. Chief Constables were sensible enough to tolerate Lambert's eccentric determination to lead from the front, for the simple reason that he got results. Bert Hook had been at his side for a decade, supplementing the 'guv'nor's' strengths with his own sturdy qualities, refusing the promotion to Inspector rank that would surely have been his due because he was happy in the niche he had built for himself under Lambert's direction.

On the golf course, it was proving a different matter for the newly arrived Hook. The two now played the last few holes in a simmering silence, while Bert's score and temper mounted in inexorable tandem. John Lambert watched his Sergeant's broad, weatherbeaten features growing ever redder and marvelled that such an equable man should be so near to losing control of himself. Then, on the eighteenth, Lambert went into a bunker, took two to get out, and applied several epithets to his ball which did not appear in the police manual. To Bert Hook, who had long since abandoned hope for his own performance, it was a wholly satisfying episode.

After they had showered, life fell slowly back into perspective over pints of bitter and amidst hearty male badinage. There were tales of disasters worse than anything even the police duo had suffered. Bert Hook, who had heartily sworn his abandonment of the game in the ditch beside the sixteenth, agreed to play in a four-ball on the following Sunday as he left the golf club.

Eleanor Hook studied her husband's face carefully as he negotiated the Mondeo carefully round the boys' bikes on the driveway. She was hoping this new interest would give him the physical outlet he would need in the early retirement which was inevitable for policemen; Eleanor was a woman who believed in planning ahead, and most men were just big boys at heart. She let him come into the kitchen and boom out his ritual condemnation of the futility of golf and his derision for his own dismal performance before she gave him her information.

"They've been on from the station for you. A body in the churchyard at Broughton's Ash. Suspicious circumstances, they think."

Bert Hook knew what that meant. Murder, almost certainly. Back to work, then, with a vengeance. Well, it was almost a relief: anything must be better than golf.

On Monday morning, the police machinery of a murder hunt was fully in train. As yet it had turned up little of significance. House-to-house enquiries had revealed no one who had seen or heard violence in the ancient churchyard where the corpse had been discovered by the retired vicar Thomas Dodds. There were irritatingly imprecise descriptions of three vehicles which had been seen in the church lane the night before the body had been found. If it proved that the body had been dumped at the site rather than killed in the churchyard, these would need to be followed up, but the sightings were so fleeting that to date there was little more than the colour of the vehicles to be recorded.

There was no evidence yet as to the time of death; that would come from the forensic services in the next few hours. Until then, there would be no certainty even that this was murder rather than suicide, though the Scene of Crime team combing the deep grass near the wall of the cemetery had little doubt of it. Most important of all, the police had no idea of who this man with the severed throat was. Murder hunts begin with the victim and spread outwards; until the victim was identified, this killing dwelt in a limbo of uncertainty.

Detective Inspector Christopher Rushton had been quietly confident that he would have the victim identified within the hour. But his computer scans of first the local and then the national registers of missing persons had revealed no one who provided an exact match with the statistics they had already registered before the corpse was removed in its plastic shell for the forensic scientists at Chepstow to begin their work. He had jotted down a few possibilities, but none of them was local, and he had no great confidence that their man was among them.

He confessed as much to John Lambert – reluctantly, for he always liked to show off the marvels of modern technology to a man who seemed to Rushton to prefer older and clumsier methods. "Nothing as yet from the MISPA files. SOCO have brought in a print from the body, but there's no match so far. I'll be certain within another hour, but it seems he didn't have a record."

Lambert nodded. Already this one looked like falling outside the routine statistics of suspicious deaths. Four-fifths were family killings, where you could expect to have an arrest within forty-eight hours. Of the other victims, two-thirds had a criminal record of some kind. If they proved to be habitual criminals, it didn't necessarily make detection easy – gangland murders by hired killers

11

were the hardest of all to bring to court, because of the difficulties of proof – but at least you knew where to look.

"There was no identification in his pockets," said Bert Hook. "No money; no wallet; no credit cards; nothing but a stub of pencil and a soiled handkerchief." The three men stood in Lambert's office, digesting the little they had, each too experienced a CID man to voice the obvious. This might be theft, a mugging that had got out of hand when the victim resisted and the attacker panicked. Deaths or serious injuries in such circumstances were becoming increasingly common. But they were still largely confined to urban areas, and not many muggers were well enough organised to remove the body when violence overspilled into death. Mugging was a cowardly but opportunist crime; when it went wrong, the perpetrators usually took to their heels and left their victims where they had fallen.

"We've had three missing persons reported this morning, but they were all teenage girls," said Rushton. "I've put out a national alert for any men around forty who've gone missing in the last seventy-two hours. I'll add a more accurate description later in the day."

When forensic had been able to add some details, that meant, and all of them knew it. As if answering a cue, the phone on Lambert's desk shrilled urgently. "This is Dr Saunders, Home Office Pathology Lab at Chepstow," said a thin, rather querulous voice. "Do I have Detective Superintendent John Lambert?" Lambert affirmed his identity and motioned his companions to stay put. He could picture Dr Saunders, behind the desk where he had once clashed with him on a previous case,* a thin man with a tightly trimmed beard, an academic more at home with things than people. Dr Saunders was a scientist who had chosen pathology because it was a more exact science than surgery, where you dealt with live flesh and pulsing blood.

"I have your man on the table now, but I haven't begun the investigation proper. You'll have my full report by tomorrow morning, but I thought you might like a few preliminary facts," said the reedy voice. It sounded as if it was already regretting this voluntary stepping beyond the bounds of protocol.

Lambert hastily reassured him. "That is very thoughtful, Dr Saunders. It will also be most useful. We haven't yet identified our victim, you see. Until we do, it's difficult to begin a proper attempt to establish the facts of his death."

"I see." Saunders sounded encouraged. "Well, I can confirm what you already knew fairly certainly. Your man was murdered. People do cut their own throats still, and it's not unknown for suicides to choose churchyards for the act, but this man didn't. His throat wasn't cut, in fact. He was garrotted, probably taken from behind with a thin wire."

Lambert, scribbling furiously upon the pad in front of him, gave an involuntary sigh. "Any great strength involved?"

"No. With the implement used, this could easily have been done by a woman – even a child, if the victim was

* See *Girl Gone Missing*.

13

taken by surprise." Saunders' voice carried a curious satisfaction, as though the notion cheered him up. Then, as if to dispel any such impression, he moved hastily into routine facts. "Your man was five feet eleven inches tall and weighed sixty-seven kilograms – twelve stones and three pounds if you prefer it. I would compute his age as late thirties. He had fair hair, recently cut and styled, and the body was in good condition."

"Any evidence of a struggle?"

"At first glance, no. There is no sign of skin or fibres under the fingernails, but that is as far as I can go. I haven't examined the body skin in any detail yet."

They knew what he meant. It was routine now to check the inner thighs and buttocks of men as well as women for any signs of sexual assault, any traces of semen.

Lambert said, "Thank you for taking the trouble to ring me, Dr Saunders. We look forward to your full report in due course."

In truth, the pathologist's early call hadn't taken them much further forward. But there were a few more details to ink in on the picture of their mystery man. He was well nourished, and had thought enough of his appearance to have his hair expensively cut and shaped. Not a vagrant, then: no need at present to trawl the meths drinkers and other dropouts who lived precariously in the twilight world of the homeless.

Lambert hated this quiet period, with a murder team and its machinery in place, routine enquiries begun, and yet no clear focus for the work. It was like a phoney war, where everyone waited for the real battles to commence in a state of uneasy mental excitement. For John Lambert admitted that he was excited: he was too old a hand now to feel any guilt about the zest for the hunt which was a part of any CID man's temperament.

Because there was nothing more to be done yet, he went home for lunch. Christine made him a sandwich with her usual speed and dexterity, but she looked grey with fatigue. She had to force the smile she gave him when she caught him studying her over the sports section of the paper. "I've been hoeing the front garden – last time before the winter, I expect," she said.

She had volunteered the explanation for her tiredness before he had voiced the question. It wasn't like her even to admit to physical weakness. It meant that she must feel as exhausted as she looked, he reflected. He watched her knuckles whiten with the effort of raising herself from the armchair as she levered her frame into action. She taught part-time now in the local primary school a mile from their door, having volunteered to give up her full-time post when falling rolls in the schools determined that some teachers must go.

As he watched her reverse her small car carefully between the gateposts, he was glad again that she had agreed to cut down the work she had always loved to a part-time commitment. It was clearly enough for her now. Well, neither of them was getting any younger; he tried to console himself with the meaningless cliché he remembered his own parents voicing a generation ago. But even as he smiled sourly at that recollection, he knew that there was more to it than that.

He examined the heavy clay soil of the front garden as

15

he went back to his car. The area of soil newly disturbed by hoeing was pitifully small.

PC Bryn Jones made a routine check on the school at two thirty, driving slowly past in his patrol car. A visible presence, they called it. As far as he was concerned, it was as important to be noticed by the old busybody who had reported the suspicious presence as by the man himself. There wasn't much kudos to be gained by bringing in paedophiles, anyway. But of this one, real or imagined, there was no sign.

PC Jones stopped for a moment to watch the girls playing hockey, checking that the pavements for three hundred yards to either side of him were deserted. Mind you, perverts were as likely to be watching the boys playing football these days, he reflected, from the wisdom and experience of his twenty-two years. No accounting for tastes, there wasn't. Now that full-chested girl who had just burst through and scored a goal, she'd be a right cracker in two or three years, mind . . .

PC Jones thought suddenly of his mother and the Bethesda Chapel Sunday School, and drove hastily away.

He returned just before the bell ended afternoon school at four o'clock. There were many cars now in the street that had been deserted; he parked the police car as unobtrusively as he could at the end of the line, then strolled down to the ragged crowd of mothers, grandmothers and grandfathers who stood outside the school gates on that pleasantly warm autumn afternoon. It was impossible not to be noticed in uniform, of course. Bryn

16

Jones, who had dreams of a transfer to CID in due course, imagined himself blending discreetly with this polyglot assembly of humanity, picking up vital information about serious crime as he passed among them.

Instead, his uniform brought him curious glances, nervous nods of acknowledgement, even a series of giggles from some of the women in conversation on the periphery of the mass. He was sure he was the centre of their hilarity, though he could not imagine why. He felt the blush he always feared would undermine his authority creeping from his collar up into his cheeks.

He was relieved when the children poured in a raucous tide of blue uniforms from the school and distracted attention from him. He resumed his task of looking for any odd man who was submerging himself among the crowd of parents and grandparents, hoping to pass unnoticed and wait here to prey upon unaccompanied children as they walked away from the school into the November dusk. He found nothing suspicious; either the call had been a false alarm from an overheated imagination, or the mysterious man had been warned off by the police presence. Or it might be that this was an elderly man who simply liked children, in a perfectly innocent way; that was much more common than an uncharitable society which fed upon sensationalism cared to admit.

The children shrilled their goodbyes to each other as they went their separate ways. Jones gathered bits of school news, most of it unintelligible to him. But one piece of information he heard three times. Old Gilesy was off – they'd had mayhem for one lesson because no one had realised at first that he was missing. Apparently Old

Murray had been livid about it. Bryn Jones was near enough to his own school days to remember that every teacher was "old" to his young charges. And he knew that "Old Murray" was the man in charge of this establishment, for a board not five yards to his right proclaimed in gold lettering that T. H. Murray, MA, was the Head Teacher of Oldford County Secondary School.

Bryn Jones had no idea who Old Gilesy was, but the fact that he was missing caught his attention. And the fact that no one seemed to know why made him very interested indeed. For PC Bryn Jones had heard at the station that the MISPA files had been trawled unsuccessfully in search of the identity of the body discovered after the Remembrance Day service in Broughton's Ash churchyard. It was a long shot, but you never knew . . .

There is much to be said for youthful enthusiasm. PC Jones marched with determination into the school, ignoring the derisive remarks from the older boys behind him. He was told by the Head's secretary that Mr Murray was conducting a short meeting with three of his senior staff and must not be disturbed, but PC Jones announced loftily that this was urgent police business and must take precedence. He was through the outer office and rapping on the Head Teacher's door before the outraged dragon who guarded it could prevent him. He surprised himself sometimes, did Bryn.

Thomas Murray, MA, seemed more disturbed to see a policeman than a headmaster should, and Bryn had his questions ready. "I understand that you have a Mr Giles on your staff."

"Yes. Edward Giles. He teaches Chemistry. When he's here."

"I see. But he has not been here today?"

"No. It was very inconvenient, in fact. The laboratories, you see. They're not like ordinary classrooms. You can't just let children—"

"Do you know where Mr Giles is, Mr Murray?" Bryn tried to keep the rising excitement out of his voice.

"No. That's what was so inconsiderate. Normally people ring in if they're ill, or at least—"

"You haven't heard from him all day?" PC Jones tried to keep it impersonal, but he knew he had spoken abruptly. The answer to this could mean a real feather in his cap. The mysterious, exciting world of CID beckoned beguilingly.

"No. It's a real nuisance, I don't mind telling you. I've just spoken to my Deputy Head, and we don't know whether to cover his classes for tomorrow or not. If only—"

"I think I must ask you to come to the station with me, Mr Murray. Immediately, please."

This time PC Jones made no attempt to disguise his satisfaction.

It was two hours later that Bert Hook took a shaken and embarrassed Thomas Murray to the Murder Room which had been hastily set up in Oldford police station. The headmaster had not enjoyed his meeting with his old adversary* Superintendent John Lambert. This grave

* See *Girl Gone Missing*.

19

inquisitor with the long face and the steel-grey hair knew things about Murray that neither his staff nor his governors knew. Although on this occasion Tom Murray had nothing to hide, he felt that his answers were being weighed and found wanting, as though he was an unreliable witness. It was a relief to be led away from Lambert's office by the bluff and solid Sergeant Hook.

"We shall need a formal identification of the corpse by a near relative in due course," explained Hook. "It isn't even available for inspection at the moment, but we do have a photograph of the dead man's face, taken by our Scene of Crime photographer. It would be helpful if you could either confirm it as Mr Giles, or eliminate him from our enquiries."

Tom Murray, who was anxious only to have the matter done with and be away from there, could nevertheless not prevent a start of horror as he stared at the shut eyes and sallow features of the face he had seen so often in animated life. His breath came in uneven gasps as he said, "That's him all right. That's Ted Giles."

The murder investigation had a focus.

Three

M ick Yates tried to keep a low profile in the school. He wasn't used to being summoned to the Head's office. When he was asked to go there immediately after school assembly on the morning of Tuesday, 13th November, he wondered what on earth he could have done wrong. After five minutes of wracking his pessimistic brain in the outer office, he found that the explanation was more outlandish than anything he had imagined.

Tom Murray came out of his office with two large men at his heels. His face filled with relief when he saw Mick. He said to the men, "This is Michael Yates. Superintendent Lambert and Sergeant Hook, Michael. They need to ask a few questions about one of our colleagues and I said you were the man best equipped to help them. You can use my office – I'll go and see to your class."

Murray bustled away, scarcely troubling to disguise his relief, and Mick, after hesitating for a moment, led the men back into the holy of holies that was the Head Teacher's office. He had been in there only once before. He could not bring himself to take the head's seat, the big swivel chair behind the green leather top of the desk. Instead, he pulled a stand chair from the wall and sat upon it awkwardly, like a pupil who had been brought in here for a lecture. In the end, no one took the head's seat. The two detectives pulled armchairs round to face him, Mick realised now that he had left himself facing the light, whilst his interrogators had their backs to it; perhaps he had read too many thrillers.

Lambert gave him a small, encouraging smile. "Do you know why we're here, Mr Yates?"

"No. I've no idea." He couldn't think of anything he'd done. Nothing to bring out top brass like Superintendents, anyway. They didn't send people like that to chase up overdue MOTs: he knew that much about the police.

"You know that a colleague of yours, Edward Giles, has been missing?"

Mick had never heard him called anything but Ted before, just as no one in the school had called him Michael until the head had introduced him to these two. This formality seemed somehow ominous. "I know Ted wasn't in yesterday. I covered one of his classes for him. I'm a biologist and he's a biochemist, really, but we both teach Life Sciences as well as our own specialisms." He felt himself talking too much, as if trying to postpone the real issues. Their next words confirmed the thought.

It was the muscular, slightly overweight one, the Sergeant, who said quietly, "When did you last see Mr Giles, Michael?"

Mick thought furiously. The Sergeant seemed friendly, had used his first name. But wasn't there some kind of system they used, when working in pairs – hard cop, friendly cop, or something like that? You mustn't let them trick you into a mistake. And perhaps Ted was in some kind of trouble. "Friday, it would be, after school."

"Did he give you any idea of how he proposed to spend the weekend?"

"No. I don't think we even spoke. I was anxious to get away quickly that night: the ninth is my wife's birthday." He found himself bursting into a nervous smile, revelling in the display of a perfectly innocent fact to the Superintendent, whose grey eyes had never left his face since he sat down.

It was Lambert who now gave him the information which stunned him, coldly, evenly, studying him for the effect it might have. "I have to tell you that your colleague was found dead in Broughton's Ash churchyard on Sunday morning, Mr Yates. The circumstances of his death were suspicious. That's why we're here this morning. We need to piece together a picture of Ted Giles's last hours. We're told that you are the person in the school who knew him best."

As Mick's mind reeled, his first impulse was to distance himself from this. Murder, they meant. The very word pushed him so far out of his depth that he was floundering. "Oh, no! Well, I suppose it might be true – that I knew him best of the staff in the school, I mean. But you see, no one knew him very well. He kept himself pretty much to himself."

Lambert wondered why this open-faced young man was so defensive. Could this young innocent possibly have anything to hide? But his reaction, while irrational if he was guiltless, was not so uncommon. People still shied away from the oldest and gravest

23

crime of all. He said, "How long had you known Ted Giles, Mr Yates?"

Already the past tense, Mick noted. He gathered his resources. He had nothing to fear, surely; he must help these earnest professionals to find out who had done this to Ted. "Since I came to the school, three years ago in September. He showed me the ropes, told me how to handle – well, how to behave with senior staff. There was some overlap in our teaching, as I've said, and he helped me with the exam syllabuses."

"And what about your lives outside the school? Did you meet much socially?"

"Not really. Ted was separated from his wife. We used to go for a drink together sometimes – usually after a parent–teacher evening or a staff meeting, things like that. We didn't have a regular night."

Hook took up the questioning again. He had a notebook in front of him now. "We need to know as much as we can about the victim when there's a murder. I'm sure you understand that, Michael."

"It's Mick. Everyone calls me Mick." It suddenly seemed important, as though it would have been dishonest to let them go on calling him Michael when Ted Giles never had.

"Mick, then. We know practically nothing yet about Ted Giles, so anything you can tell us will be valuable at this stage. He was a little older than you, wasn't he?"

"Yes. I'm thirty-two now. Ted was nearly forty, I think. He was a good teacher, firm with the kids, but easy with it. He was quite popular with them." He said it wistfully, so that Hook wondered irrelevantly whether he

24

found discipline as easy and unforced as the dead man had. "He was a good-looking man, I suppose." He said it as though it had struck him for the first time. He was accustomed, particularly in school, to assess people first and foremost in terms of teaching ability.

"And what were his sexual preferences?"

For an instant, Mick did not know what Hook meant. Then he said with a smile, "Women! Definitely. He might have lived on his own, but Ted certainly wasn't gay." He looked for a moment as if he was about to enlarge on that theme, with examples, but then thought better of it.

"Bit of a lady's man, was he?" asked Lambert gloomily. He didn't want to hear that the dead man had been a Lothario, with a long string of conquests, some of them jealous of their successors. The recluse with few contacts made the ideal murder victim, from the biased viewpoint of the CID.

"I wouldn't say that exactly. But he was a free agent; he'd been separated for a long time. I never met his wife." He added the last sentence as an afterthought, as if it had only just struck him that his friend had had a life before him.

Hook said heavily, "You'd better give us a list of the ladies involved."

"Oh, I couldn't do that. I don't know them, you see. There are girls on the staff here who would have gone out with him, I'm sure, but Ted preferred to keep his working life separate from his social life. Business and pleasure didn't mix, he always said." Actually he'd usually put it in the form of advice to his less experienced colleague. "Don't shit on your own doorstep!" he'd often told a wistful Mick when the conversation in the pub turned to sex. But Mick didn't want to put it in those terms when a police officer was taking notes; that would have seemed unfair to his dead friend, somehow. A breach of his confidence, perhaps.

Lambert sighed. "We were told you knew the late Mr Giles better than anyone else on the staff here. Yet so far it seems that you don't know very much about the life of your colleague and friend, Mr Yates."

"No. I'm afraid he was – well, quite a private sort of man, really." Mick had never thought of Ted like that before. He had been content with the older man's friendship, flattered by it, indeed. Only now did he realise how much he had told Ted of his own problems with the job and his private life, and how little Ted had released about himself.

"What about people within the school? Was he close to anyone? Did he have any enemies on the staff that you know of?"

Mick felt his pulses quickening at that thought. This was a murder inquiry. He was being asked to name people who would immediately become suspects. For a wild moment, he was tempted to name the Head of PE, who teased him so tirelessly about his Biology classes with the senior girls, but he sensed that this was not the moment for retaliatory humour. Searching desperately for something that would justify the importance he had been accorded in this case, he said, "I did once hear Ted having a row of some sort with Graham Reynolds."

"Who is?" Hook had his ball-pen poised over the still almost empty page of his notebook.

"Oh, yes, sorry. Graham Reynolds is our Head of the Social Studies Department."

"And what was the row about?"

"I don't know. It was behind closed doors, you see. In Ted's Chemistry lab. I'm sorry."

"No need to be. You can't report what you didn't hear. People who add their own speculations cause us a lot of trouble. And they always make bad witnesses in court." No harm in reminding the punters they might end up as witnesses, Bert always thought. It sharpened their minds wonderfully on occasions. "So you heard what we shall call a heated exchange." He wrote the phrase down with satisfaction in his large hand, playing up the village bobby image which had caught out so many villains in the past. "And this was behind the doors of the Chemistry laboratory. And when did this exchange take place?"

Mick cudgelled his brains desperately, anxious to offer them something of interest. "It would be about a fortnight ago. Yes – just over a fortnight, because I mentioned it to Ted when we had a drink in the pub that evening."

"And what was Ted's reaction? Did he give you any clue as to the subject of the dispute?"

"No. He just said Social Studies teachers shouldn't climb on white horses – they weren't cut out to be knights errant. I'm afraid I didn't follow that up; I got diverted, because we had a bit of a laugh about Sociology."

"Yes. People do, I understand." Hook was grave as a rubicund Buddha. No one would have known he was about to complete an Open University degree which had included a Social Studies module. He made a note about the date of this exchange, which was almost certainly irrelevant, but which would need to be followed up in due course.

Lambert said, "Is there anything else you can tell us about the life of this man? What about his habits outside the routine of his school life? Did he play any sports? Was he a member of any clubs? Was there anywhere he went regularly, say every week?"

Mick Yates listened earnestly to each prompting, then shook his head sadly. He wondered if these men would think he was concealing things, when all that was becoming apparent was that he knew so little about the life of the man whom he had thought of as a friend and mentor. "Ted went skiing every winter. Usually over New Year, I think. But I'm pretty sure he wasn't a member of any sports club. He played a bit of squash and tennis, but he wasn't a member of a club."

"How about golf?" said Hook hopefully. The dead man might be a fellow-sufferer; even better, his killer might be a golf club committee member.

"No, he wasn't interested. He said it was a game for old fogies."

Lambert didn't even flinch: you had to admire his professionalism, Hook thought. The Superintendent said rather wearily, "Habits, Mr Yates. Was there any evening or day that Ted Giles set aside for himself and his own interests?"

At first, Mick Yates looked as blank as ever. Then he brightened with a recollection. "Ted was never around on a Friday evening. I asked him out for a drink after school was over for the week quite a few times, but he always had some prior commitment on Fridays."

Detective Inspector Rushton found he got on well with Dr Saunders, the pathologist at the Home Office Forensic Science Laboratory at Chepstow.

Both men favoured facts rather than speculation; both had a liking for documentation and the logical ordering of information; both felt happier with the tabulation of facts and the scientific approach to crime than with understanding its perpetrators and its victims. Chris Rushton explained that he had come to Chepstow in an attempt to save the time that was always vital in a murder investigation rather than because he hoped to gain anything extra from a personal hearing of what would be in Cliff Saunders' confidential report.

Once an initial stiffness between the two had evaporated, Saunders found that Rushton was genuinely interested in his findings and how they might best be incorporated into the police computer system. He felt himself being drawn into the puzzles of detection, wanting to provide the best detail he could for the man beside him, who would take his findings on into the hunt for the man or woman who had perpetrated this. "Everything will be in my report, which you'll have tomorrow," he said, "But if there are any key areas, we can talk about them now."

"Time of death," said Rushton without hesitation.

"Between ten and twenty hours before he was found. You'll find the details of body temperature and the stage of rigor mortis in my report, but I'd be prepared to say in court between four p.m. on Saturday the tenth of November and two a.m. on Sunday the eleventh."

Rushton didn't push him further. Mentally, he made a note that whilst Saunders would not go further than this in court, the middle of this time period was the likeliest time for their murder – say between six and twelve on the Saturday night. Not the best time – during hours of darkness and when the police themselves would have been fully engaged with the normal tedious vandalism and violence of Saturday night drinkers.

"And where did he die?" The three questions every young DC learned to ask first about suspicious deaths: where, when and how. Saunders had already told them how and when: Rushton already suspected that the normally straightforward "Where?" was going to give them difficulty. The SOC team had indicated as much to him before he came here.

Saunders smiled grimly. "I can tell you where he didn't die. In that churchyard at Broughton's Ash."

"He was dumped there after death?"

"Yes. A few hours afterwards, I'd guess." Cliff Saunders' nose wrinkled in distaste above his neat mouth and carefully trimmed beard at the imprecision of this; he wasn't a man given to guessing. "He'd been lying face down after death for perhaps two hours; there was discernible hypostasis on the front of the body. But he was moved before there was any rigor in the limbs."

"Presumably in a vehicle of some sort?"

"Almost certainly, unless he was moved only a very short distance. But that is more your province than mine, Chris." Saunders had forced himself into the use of the forename, and it surprised both of them. "There were some scratches on the lower back which probably came from the top of that stone wall at the cemetery – as though he was levered on to it and then thrust over."

Rushton nodded. "The Scene of Crime team found some fibres from his clothing on the top of the wall. And he was lying almost against it."

"There are faint marks at the bottom of the shoulder blades which look like finger damage – consistent with someone having lugged him out of a vehicle by gripping him under the arms. There are no similar marks on the legs. Although we can't rule out the possibility that someone else took hold of that end without leaving marks, it seems unlikely."

Chris Rushton made another note to be fed into his computer within the hour: probably only one person involved in the disposal of the body after the killing. Grudgingly, he gave back a little information of his own. "It seems the dead man was a schoolteacher at Oldford Comprehensive. An Edward Giles. Separated from his wife. Lived on his own. Is there anything else you can tell us which might be of interest?"

Saunders pursed his lips. "All the detail will be in my report. There is one thing you might like to know immediately, though. Your Edward Giles had sex not long before he died."

"Lucky bugger!" It was partly the automatic reaction of a policeman in a force which was still overwhelmingly male, partly the instinctive envy from a man living alone and still coming to terms with a divorce he had never wanted.

31

Cliff Saunders gave him a mirthless smile, still mindful of the stainless-steel dishes with their covers in the room next door, each containing organs from the body he had so recently cut up. He had left them laid out methodically, like the dishes for some nightmare banquet.

"He doesn't seem too lucky to me," he said.

Four

T ed Giles's flat was as neat and clean as that of a houseproud woman. The fitted carpets were newly vacuumed. The bed was neatly made. Even in the bathroom, that most revealing of sanctums for curious coppers, the porcelain shone, and save for a clean brush and comb, everything was neatly stowed away in the mirror-fronted cupboard above the washbasin. In the kitchen, there was not a cup nor a spoon to be seen on the neat white sink. But for an occasional drip from the cold tap, this might have been a show flat, still to be occupied, rather than one in which a man had lived for five years.

Sergeant "Jack" Johnson looked around this clinically clean residence with distaste. For police teams in search of pointers, premises like this were always the least rewarding. Filth, squalor, and sloppiness in living were the allies he and his team welcomed. You rarely found anything as helpful as the bloodstains Johnson had found on the walls and the floor of the house where he had worked last week, but that was only a straightforward "domestic", where they had already made an arrest. Here, though he had his constables on hands and knees with tweezers and dishes, Johnson wasn't hopeful even of the clothing fibres and stray hairs they expected to pick up as routine trophies. Ted Giles, successful teacher, separated from his wife, and now murder victim, seemed determined to remain otherwise anonymous, even after death.

They found no diaries, of course: Giles must have been a man who carried whatever appointments he might have in his head. There was a calendar beside the spotless electric oven with a few initials against particular dates; they would take this away in due course, but he doubted if they would be anything more than dental appointments, library book return dates, and family birthdays. Johnson already had Edward Giles down as a depressingly secretive man.

He said as much to John Lambert when the chief arrived. "There's a cleaner, of course; there bloody would be! Last came in on Friday morning," he said gloomily. The efficient daily help was one of the banes of his life. The Superintendent nodded, then looked around him like an eager sniffer dog. A quarter of a century of CID experience, of entering deserted rooms of all shapes and sizes, with an infinite range of decor and contents, had not removed the curiosity which was an essential part of the professional detective. He walked into each of the two neat bedrooms, then the bathroom, then the kitchen, all within thirty seconds and without opening a cupboard or a drawer. You didn't tread on the toes of the specialists, and Johnson was a specialist whom he trusted absolutely to miss nothing.

"*Too* tidy, do you think, Jack?" he said. "Could just be that he had something in his life to hide? Not necessarily criminal, but something he preferred to conceal from whoever came into his home."

Johnson was unconvinced. "He lived alone. No wife who might go through his pockets or smell his shirts in search of other women."

"But we don't know yet who he brought here. He might have preferred to conceal parts of himself from his visitors. It's a thought for your lads and lasses. Might help to keep them going through a boring day."

Johnson nodded dolefully. "We'll bag the sheets and pillowcases and any soiled clothes, of course. Might just get DNA samples of someone if we're lucky."

Both of them glanced without much hope at the open door of the main bedroom. They both knew without further words what he meant: if at some further stage of the investigation they were able to prove the presence here of someone who denied having ever set foot in the flat, it could well be significant. And particularly so if the evidence of DNA suggested also an intimate relationship where none had been admitted.

Lambert sighed; such speculation was a reminder of how far away they were from any such candidates for the murderer of Ted Giles. He went out of the flat onto the landing outside. With its single long strip of carpet and its rows of shut doors, it was as clean and anonymous as a corridor in a private hospital. Lambert hesitated for a moment, then rapped sharply on the door immediately to the left of Ted Giles's flat.

At first, he thought no one was in. Then there were muffled movements and the door opened not more than eight inches. A broad face peered at him from beneath straight, greasy black hair. "I don't buy nothing at the door!" it mouthed.

Lambert showed his warrant card, beckoned sharply to Bert Hook, who was emerging from the lift behind him, and said, "We need to speak to you. It won't take long, Mr . . . ?"

The man refused the invitation to give his name, looked for a moment as if he would slam the door in their faces, then thought better of it. He snarled, "I got nothing to say. Not to the likes of you. I don't deal with pigs!"

The old attitude. Even the old words. Lambert put his face a little nearer, so that his grey eyes stared down into the watery brown ones beneath him. "Yes you do. Either here or at the station. When we're investigating murder, we question whoever we want to."

He took advantage of the shock the word "murder" gave even to the most hardened to push back the door and the man behind it and walk into the flat. The place smelt faintly of stale sweat and strongly of stale cigarette smoke. It was as dirty and untidy as Giles's flat had been clean and neat. The two big men looked round the living room unhurriedly, taking in the dirty curtains, the sofa with a hole where its innards threatened to escape, the cheap framed print of the negress askew upon the wall, the sink half-full of unwashed crockery. The man felt their gaze revolving like a film-maker's camera, taking in each detail, coming to rest eventually upon him and staying there.

Hook smiled at him, enjoying his discomfiture, producing a notebook to add to the man's apprehension. "I think we'll have your name for a start," he said.

The man crossed his arms across his T-shirted chest. "It's Bass," he said. "Aubrey Bass." He looked at them aggressively, as if he expected the first name to be a source of derision; no doubt his novelettish handle had often caused mirth in the circles he inhabited. When the name provoked no reaction in Hook, he scratched himself vigorously, first under one arm, then under the other, then under both at the same time. When both the policemen observed this action impassively and neither of them spoke, the man did not know what else to do. Realising he could not scratch for ever, he dropped his right hand to his side and they saw that the lettering on his T-shirt spelled out *Fulham for the Cup*. The lettering was a little smeared and the originally white background was mapped with a variety of interesting stains, as though reflecting the ridiculous ambition of the slogan.

Bass thought he saw Lambert's gaze straying to the telly, which he knew was hooky. "Well, waddyerwant?" he said roughly.

"A little information, that's all, Aubrey," said Hook.

Bass looked at him suspiciously, searching for any note of mockery in the intonation of his first name. "I don't give no information, not to the filth," he said roughly.

But it was a token response. His aggression had drained away with his nerve in the silences they had visited upon him. "You'll help us with this, if you know what's good for you," said Lambert brusquely. He looked the man full in the face, taking in his unshaven appearance, his unbrushed teeth, his face graining with sweat as his fingers began to scratch anew, this time at the tattoo on his left forearm.

"I don't know nothing about no murder," he said.

Lambert smiled, wondering whether this plethora of negatives was an unconscious attempt to emphasise his ignorance. "Perhaps not. We shall see. What can you tell us about your neighbour, Mr Giles?" he said.

Bass relaxed visibly, sank into the armchair beside the empty fireplace, and gestured towards the erupting sofa. If it was that stuck-up bugger next door they were interested in, they couldn't be here about any of his own little interests. "Ted Giles? I don't see much of him."

The answer came automatically: this man's instinct was not to help the police. But it might well be true; Bass might be as unlike Giles as the condition of their flats indicated. They had certainly lived in very different ways. But this unattractive creature might still know things of interest about the dead man. Lambert said, "We need to know about whatever you've seen of Mr Giles in the last few months. All of it."

Bass shrugged his heavy shoulders, scratched again, this time at his stomach with his left hand. Hook, perched on the edge of the sofa beside John Lambert, glanced nervously at the material beside him; fleas were an occupational hazard when you came into places like this. Bass said reluctantly, "We 'ad a drink once – when I first came here, two years ago. But he wouldn't go out with me again." While Hook reflected that this was rather in the dead man's favour, Bass's heavy features turned even more sullen at the recollection. Then they suddenly brightened. "In trouble, is he? Must be, to bring a superintendent round 'ere. Hey, you mentioned murder. He's never—"

"Mr Giles is the victim, not the criminal. We're questioning everyone who was close to him."

Aubrey Bass would never have made a success of serious villainy. He was far too transparent. His jaw dropped. "Young Giles is dead? And you're . . . 'Ere, you can't possibly think I'ad anything to do with—"

"Where were you on Saturday night, Aubrey?" Hook let a little contempt seep into the name this time. He didn't seriously think this small-time loser would be involved in murder, but there was no harm in frightening him into cooperation.

Panic filled the widening, bloodshot eyes. "Round at a friend's. We went to a couple of pubs first, then back to his place. We had a bevvy, a few laughs, a game of cards."

"Good. You can give us the exact times and the place. And the names of your friends. I'm sure they'll be only too anxious to help the police." Hook made an entry in his notebook and beamed down at it with satisfaction. "Now, tell us everything you know about the late Ted Giles, your ex-neighbour."

"Well, there isn't much to tell, honestly there isn't. I was only in his flat once. Went to see if 'e 'ad a few cans of lager, when we'd run out, but 'e 'adn't."

"And did Mr Giles come in here much?" said Lambert.

"Never."

That was probably true, they thought. A man who kept his living space as clinically tidy as Giles was not going to step into this tip unless he had to. "But you must know something about his way of life, living as close as you did," said Hook, a little desperately.

"He was a teacher. At Oldford Comprehensive, I think." Bass brightened at this, even ceased scratching for a moment. It was so eminently safe.

Lambert sighed. "We know that. We also know his height, his weight and his age. We know that he lived here alone. We also know how he died. But nothing else. You must at least know something of his comings and goings."

"Not much. These walls are pretty thick, for modern places. You'd be surprised."

Thrusting away an image of this monument to hygiene crouching with his ear to a glass against the bedroom wall, Hook leaned forward a little further on the edge of the sofa. "Never mind the estate agent bit, Aubrey. Tell us whatever you know about Ted Giles. Without any more buggering about."

"Well, there isn't much I can tell you – 'onest there isn't. But 'e did 'ave a few visitors."

"That's more like it. What kind of visitors?"

This time it was Bass who leaned forward, confidentially. He had a full range of scratches, thought Lambert; this one, cross-handed to each side of his ample belly, was positively lecherous. " 'E were a bit of a lad, you know, were Ted. 'E 'ad women in there. Quite often."

Lambert leaned forward, resisting a sudden temptation to send up Bass's leer with an even more extravagant one. "The same woman, do you think? Or more than one?"

"Oh, more than one, I'm sure. Several." Aubrey Bass dwelt on that word with satisfaction, as though it was the height of linguistic sophistication, as for him it possibly was. Then he slipped back into phrases which were more familiar to him. " 'E put it about a bit, did Ted, I can tell you! Not arf!" He confirmed the information with an even more extravagant leer, which almost culminated in a wink. "I spoke to one of them a couple of times. Young, slim piece. Could 'ave done 'er a bit of good, if she'd let me, I can tell you!"

Lambert stood up quickly, anxious that Bass's nudge in the ribs should remain merely metaphorical. "Can you give us any names?"

He couldn't, of course. Even Hook's mixture of cajolery and threats could draw no more out of him, and eventually they were certain that this little was all he knew. He stood at the door as they left, scratching his chest with satisfaction. "Be able to clean up a bit now!" he said unconvincingly, as though they had held him back from the work.

Hook turned back to him. "There's about as much chance of that, Aubrey Bass, as of Fulham winning the Cup!" he said magisterially.

They had got little from this deplorable neighbour, and that little was depressing. Lambert and Hook, like most policemen, strove for a neutral moral stance. People who "put it about a bit" must look after their own consciences.

But they invariably made difficult corpses for CID men.

*   *   *

At Oldford School, the Head of the Social Sciences Department dismissed his last class of the day and looked out of the window at a school drive swarming with the noisy exuberance of children released.

The waiting was getting on Graham Reynolds' nerves, and more so now that the day was over and he had no classes in front of him to compel his attention. There had been a policeman and a policewoman making discreet enquiries among Ted Giles's pupils at lunch time. And the top brass had already been in to see Mick Yates first thing this morning, after assembly. He knew that, though the young man had never said anything to him about it during the rest of the day.

They must know about him. They would come eventually, he was sure. He went into the staff room, forced himself into the usual banter, the usual humorous binding about the job. He marked a few essays, used the kettle to make a cup of tea, watched the phone in the corner for the summons he knew must surely come. When he went out to his car, he pulled up his coat collar against the cool night air, as if concealing himself from hidden watchers.

Sociologists were often reviled for having all the answers. Graham Reynolds hadn't. He was a worried man.

The light was dying on what had never been a bright day. Bert Hook looked as though he was nervous about being seen, even in this light. He peered nervously over his shoulder for hidden witnesses to his shame as they carried the buckets of golf balls onto the astroturf platforms of the driving range.

"Just relax," said John Lambert cheerfully to his protégé.

Bert felt about as relaxed as a stripper's G-string. "Wouldn't I be better just hitting these on my own?" he said. "Getting the feel of the shot, like you said." He had refused to book lessons with the pro, since that would have acknowledged some sort of commitment to this ridiculous game, and he still didn't want to admit to that. Now, with Lambert striding at his shoulder like an anxious parent, the pro suddenly seemed much the lesser of two evils.

"Nonsense!" the Superintendent said breezily. "By all means have a few practice swings, to get your rhythm going, but I'll be ready to help as soon as you need me. Only wish I'd had an experienced player willing to help me when I began the game!"

Why does he have to be so bloody cheerful all the time? thought Bert. He's not normally like that; does he think it's part of his instructor's role?

Lambert did, though hardly consciously. He regarded himself as a teacher manqué, though his irreverent daughters had said he was more of a manky teacher whenever he had voiced the notion. Well, dear old Bert would have the benefit of the pedagogic talents and patience he had never been able to exercise. "Don't be too long warming up!" he commanded breezily. "The light's going fast."

Bert sneaked a ball onto the tee and gave it a whack, but Lambert whirled at the sound and came over to lean on the edge of the stall whence Hook was playing. He gave a cheerful smile of encouragement; to Hook, glan-

43

cing up apprehensively after he had teed the next ball, it seemed in the half-light like a goblin grin of anticipation. "In your own time," said Lambert happily.

Bert addressed the ball, feeling suddenly like an arthritic crab under this unblinking scrutiny. He was beginning his backswing when Lambert said sharply, "Are you *really* happy with that grip?"

Bert was. It had hit him a few sixes in his time on the grounds of Herefordshire and Gloucestershire. Lambert shook his head sadly and entwined his fingers into a network which Bert was sure he would never be able to repeat for himself. "Now try," said Lambert.

Bert did. The ball remained obstinately on its peg as the clubhead flashed over it. Lambert roared with laughter to tell his charge he should not be embarrassed. Bert wondered how many years you would get for manslaughter under extreme provocation. But with this grip, he might even miss as large a target as John Lambert, he thought miserably.

He got the ball away. Lambert criticised its direction. After three more attempts, he got one away straight. Lambert said it hadn't gone high enough. Bert eventually got one away straight and high. Lambert took away his 7-iron and said he was now ready for something more ambitious. Bert said with savage irony that he was lucky to have someone so perceptive at his side. Lambert agreed.

Lambert twisted Bert's shoulders and pushed his hips into the appropriate position. "We're building up your swing plane," he assured his charge. Bert counted the diminishing number of balls, concentrating on that single factor: it was his only gleam of hope in this dark world.

Malice Aforethought

With only three balls to go, the accident happened. Bert caught the ball flush at the bottom of his swing with the 4-iron which had given him so much trouble. The ball soared high, long, and straight, disappearing from his range of vision in what was admittedly now a very dim light. There was an interval of at least three seconds, as he stood back and gasped, then waited for the inevitable words of acknowledgement and praise from his delighted mentor.

Then Bert heard a tut-tutting behind him from Lambert. "What on earth happened to your follow-through that time? Just look at where the club has finished! And look where your feet have finished!"

From somewhere in the recesses of Hook's subconcious, there surfaced an old tale he had read of Wilfred Rhodes coaching a youngster in the cricket nets of long ago. *"And thee look where t'bloody ball's finished!"* he yelled. He dropped the iron and stalked away, leaving Lambert alone with his thoughts and the last two balls.

Five

T he wife of the late Edward Giles made herself up with care and waited for the CID men to come at the appointed time. At eight thirty, she felt perfectly composed, but she noticed how much more nervous she became as the time crept round to nine fifteen. By the time she saw the dark blue Scorpio easing up the drive of her house, she trembled with a trepidation she had been determined she would not feel at the prospect of this exchange.

Yet when she opened the door to Lambert and Hook, they saw a well-groomed woman in an Armani suit, who appeared composed and in control of her emotions. In the spacious drawing room, with its windows looking over vistas of weedless grass and borders where roses still gave a few brave flowers, she waved them towards a settee whose tapestried elegance could scarcely have been a greater contrast to Aubrey Bass's sprouting sofa. "I'm sorry I was away when this happened," she said. "No doubt you would have preferred to see me earlier."

"Yes. We like to speak to the next of kin first, whenever possible. In this case it wasn't. I trust the Irish police broke the news as well as these things can be done – there isn't any easy way." Lambert, through the conventional words, was studying her closely.

"They were as diplomatic and as caring as you would expect the Irish to be. They're a warm-hearted people, despite their political troubles," said Sue Giles. She threw in the clichés readily enough, suspecting that even this grizzled detective Lambert might be thrown a little by her if she could preserve this apparent serenity. "Would you care for a coffee? It's a little too soon after breakfast for me, but no doubt you both begin work early."

"No coffee, thank you. We have to make up for lost time – normally, as I said, we should have already interviewed the spouse of a suspicious death, as our first move in the investigation."

It came out like the rebuke he had not intended, but it did not ruffle Sue Giles. "Of course. I identified the body as that of my husband last night. You are convinced, then, that Ted was killed by person or persons unknown. That's the jargon, isn't it? That's what you mean by a suspicious death?"

"That is the phrase that will probably be used in the Coroner's Court, yes. Unless, of course, we have found who did this by the time of the inquest." Lambert found that he was less confident than usual, despite all his experience. When you came expecting grief, prepared to walk on eggshells of diplomacy, it was disconcerting to find a calm widow, bringing herself up to date with their progress, ticking off the identification of the remains of her dead husband as if it was no more than one item in a list of household tasks.

Sue Giles looked at him coolly. "And do you think you

will have a man arrested for the murder of Ted before the inquest?"

"It's possible. We are pursuing several lines of enquiry." Yet he knew as he spoke that both of them realised it was most unlikely. Stonewalling techniques were not likely to be effective with this woman. "We shall need the full details of your stay in Ireland at the weekend."

"Yes. We were in Killarney. We flew to Shannon Airport on Friday night."

"We?"

She looked for the first time slightly disconcerted, as if she had made her first tiny mistake in the game she had set up for herself with them. "I spent the weekend with a male companion, Mr Lambert. He flew back to Heathrow on Sunday night, but I stayed on with friends until yesterday." The small smile she allowed herself was edged with mockery. "I have been separated from Ted for five years, you know. The important thing from your point of view was that I was several hundred miles away in Éire when he was killed."

Lambert answered her smile with one of his own, trying to mirror exactly her degree of sardonic amusement. "And how do you know exactly when your husband was killed, Mrs Giles?"

"I don't. But I read in yesterday's paper that the body had been found in Broughton's Ash churchyard shortly after the Remembrance Day service on Sunday. I naturally presumed that Ted died on the Saturday night – indeed, that is the impression I was given when I went to identify the body. Are you telling me that I was misinformed?" She looked at him confidently, even challengingly, her head a little on one side, her expensively cut red-brown hair framing a face that was handsome rather than pretty, with its strong nose and clear, blue-green eyes.

"I think you are very well informed, Mrs Giles. I am reassured by it. We need to ask you some questions, you see. We are engaged in filling in the background of a murder victim. You have already showed us one important fact: that we can eliminate you from any direct involvement in your husband's death." He emphasised the word "direct" lightly, enough he hoped to plant the idea that she was not completely in the clear yet. She must have picked it up, but she looked neither irritated nor threatened. "However, we need to know something of your own relationship with him, as well as your knowledge of any other associations he had."

"There was no animosity between Ted and me. Our marriage had failed. We both came to terms with that several years ago." For the first time, she seemed a little on edge. Embarrassment, he wondered, or something more? These terse pronouncements had the air of a prepared statement. But why not? Not many people took kindly to having their private affairs exposed to a stranger, and however dispassionate she might choose to appear now, any marriage which had failed had its own saga of blazing emotions and scarred aspirations which were better not revisited.

Lambert said, "Forgive me for saying so, but you do not seem to be overwhelmed with sorrow by your husband's death."

"That's my business!"

"And mine, too. This is a murder inquiry, Mrs Giles."

He had ruffled her, for the first time, as he intended. Rage, like any other emotion, makes concealment more difficult. She said tensely, "All right. I see that. And you're right. I ceased to love Ted – if I ever did – a long time ago now. The way he lived his life was no longer my concern. That doesn't mean that I don't want you to find the man who killed him."

"Or woman. We are assured that the method used requires no great physical strength." Lambert looked down at the hands which twisted against each other in the lap of her suit. Then he lifted his gaze to the now tense face above them. "You mention the way he lived his life. That is what we are trying to piece together, Mrs Giles, and perhaps you can help us. Do you know, for instance, if he had any serious relationships at the time of his death?"

Sex: a tricky subject with an ex-wife. You left the orientation question open nowadays. There was nothing so far to indicate that Giles had not been heterosexual, but you mustn't leap to conclusions. Sue Giles seemed to have no doubts. "There were other women. None serious enough to be regarded as a lasting partnership, so far as I'm aware. But I warned you: I kept out of his affairs."

"Nevertheless, unless some serious attachment had developed quite recently, you would probably have been aware of it."

She weighed the statement carefully: she was fast regaining her composure. "Yes. I think that's probably fair. But, as I said, I was no longer interested in his

51

actions, or his attachments." There was a little flash of contempt on the last phrase, and he wondered if she was really as detached as she pretended from the life of her late husband.

"And if he *had* formed any serious attachment, that would not have upset you?"

A flash of temper blazed for a moment in the blue-green eyes. To his disappointment, she controlled it before she spoke. "I thought I had made myself clear, Superintendent. My husband's affairs were no longer my concern. I should have been delighted to hear he had found himself some liaison which was going to last." This time there was a contempt she did not trouble to conceal on the last assertion.

"And yet you chose not to divorce him."

This time she could not control her emotion. "Who the hell gave you the right to say that? What makes you think I'm going to—"

"I told you. This is a murder investigation. I have to find out how the victim lived his life. A man none of my team knows. A man none of us had even heard of until his body was found in a village churchyard. So don't talk to me about rules, about what I can and can't do, Mrs Giles. There are no rules to stop me seeking the knowledge we need about your late husband. For one thing, I owe it to him to find out who killed him. And we will find out, Mrs Giles!" He spoke evenly, but with a passion which surprised even himself. The last assertion, he knew, was mere rhetoric, an expression of determination rather than of a real certainty that they were going to make an arrest.

But passion convinced more than logic, as it often will. Sue Giles looked at him with widening eyes, then dropped her gaze before the intensity of his determination. "All right. I accept you need to know all about Ted. I just hadn't realised that this was going to involve so much of my own life – I thought I'd done with him. But I accept that murder makes its own rules. I shall tell you whatever I can."

"Thank you. I was asking you why you were not divorced from your husband."

"You should ask him that!" The words flew out in temper before she could control them, and her hand flashed instinctively to her mouth. "I'm sorry. I wish you could ask him, though. He might give you a more cogent explanation than I can."

Lambert looked through the long windows of the elegant room to the garden which dropped gently away to a large pond with a fountain playing in the centre. A modern house with at least six bedrooms and a well-tended garden of around an acre. Any divorce settlement would surely have left Ted Giles a rich man. Was it the wife who had resisted it, knowing what it would cost, knowing that she might even have to move out of this opulent place? He said, "Are you saying there was a dispute between you over the terms of the divorce?"

Sue Giles smiled bitterly. "Not over the terms, Superintendent. Over the very idea. Ted said he didn't believe in divorce. 'To have and to hold' and all that stuff."

If it was true, the dead man had been depriving himself of a fortune, by the look of this place. But he couldn't have resisted for ever against the modern divorce laws.

Perhaps he had been increasing his bargaining power by holding out, refusing to make things easy until the price was right. He said, "But you say you had been separated for five years. Even if you thought at first that you might get back together, that is ample time to have instituted divorce proceedings."

"Yes. I suppose I thought that Ted would see reason, in the end. And although I knew our marriage was finished and would have liked to see it formally terminated, it was not a matter of great importance to me until quite recently."

She looked quite calm again as she said this, as if she had always known in her heart that she would be saying it. Even the words had a prepared ring to them. Lambert offered the question they invited. "But your own circumstances have changed?"

"Indeed they have." She could not keep a little elation out of her voice, even in this strange context. "I have developed a serious attachment over the last few months. In due course, I should like to be free to marry again."

"I see. In ordinary circumstances, that would be entirely your own affair. In the present ones, you must see that we need to know the name of this man."

She smiled at them, looking very attractive now, her strong features softened by love, her tension gone with the release of its declaration. She studied the serious, attentive faces of the two men opposite her for a moment. "You really don't know yet, do you? I thought you might have picked it up when you went into Ted's school. My man is the Head of Social Sciences there, Graham Reynolds."

*   *   *

DI Chris Rushton and George Taylor, manager of the Oldford branch of the National Westminster Bank, enjoyed the preliminaries to the release of information about the late Edward Giles's account. They were both men who were used to observing the formalities their work required, both men who knew the rules and were happy to play life by them.

Taylor made his little speech about the confidentiality of the details of personal finance; Rushton responded with his speech about serious crime and the way it overrode the normal boundaries. Taylor said the crime would need to be very serious indeed to cause him to reveal the details of a client's account; Rushton said that this was as serious as it could be, as the police were now certain that Edward Giles was a homicide victim. It was like a minuet in words, with the parties advancing and retreating with the set steps they had known for years. Without any word as brutal as murder being used, the formalities were completed and Taylor graciously revealed the details of the late teacher's account.

Giles's salary from the Gloucestershire Local Education Authority came in regularly at the end of the month. There were unexceptional direct debits for payment of mortgage, gas, electricity, Council Tax and water. It was difficult to see any variations to the standard pattern which might be of interest to the police in the sheets of computer-printed figures.

Unless you went back over three or four years, which Rushton diligently did. George Taylor watched him with patient interest, wondering how long it would be before this man who seemed as diligent as he was himself came up with the query. It took a little time, of course, for a detective inspector could not be expected to be as swift in isolating the significant pointer as a bank manager. Taylor watched the neatly cut dark hair of the head bent over the paper as indulgently as if he was testing a protégé, and was almost as pleased when the DI found the significant figures.

"He's accruing money," said Rushton. "When you look at his year-end balances, he's a modest few hundred in the black at the year end until about two years ago, with income just about outstripping his outings. In these last two years, he's accrued ten thousand pounds."

"Yes. I suggested to him only a month ago that he should be thinking about investments if he had no plans to spend his balance."

"Where did the extra come from? Did he get a big salary increase?"

"No. The salary increments in the last two years are barely ahead of inflation. You need to look in a little more detail at those last two years."

Lambert and most other policemen would have demanded brusquely that the manager stopped playing games and told him the secrets he plainly already understood. But Rushton pored obediently over the sheets of the last months of Ted Giles's financial life, enjoying the puzzle. After little more than a minute, he looked up at his mentor's amused, indulgent face, a pupil who had found the answer and expected to be praised. "He's stopped withdrawing money for everyday expenses," he said. "The incomings from his salary and the outgoings on his standard orders have risen a little in tandem, but in the last two years he has almost ceased to withdraw money for his own purposes from the account."

"Correct," said George Taylor delightedly.

"Why?"

The bank manager's face fell. "That is not my concern. It is – was – Mr Giles's own business."

"Well, it's our concern," said Rushton. "Got to be, now. He had to be getting money from somewhere. Another account, do you think?"

George Taylor looked pained. He was white-haired, immaculate, nearing retirement. It still pained him to think of his customers using other channels for their finance, even though it might be the rule rather than the exception nowadays. "That's always possible, of course. Or he might be receiving cash payments from somewhere and spending them directly, rather than putting them into the bank. But that's rare among professional men like Mr Giles. Market traders do it – they spend to dodge tax rather than depositing the money in a bank." Despite himself, he couldn't prevent a tinge of old-fashioned class disapproval in his voice as he mentioned the market traders and their dubious financial practice.

Chris Rushton had enjoyed the formalities of his little rallies across the banking net with George Taylor, but he was in the end more detective inspector than financial conformist. He relished the abnormality in the dealings of the late Ted Giles; he had established another missing piece in this jigsaw where they had to discover the pieces for themselves. "We shall have to find where this extra income was coming from," he said with satisfaction.

* * *

It was not DI Rushton but a humble WPC who revealed the secret. A routine trawl of the list of depositors at local banks and building societies revealed a savings account in the name of the late Edward Giles at the Ross-on-Wye branch of the Halifax Building Society. It had been opened exactly two years before his death.

The young woman who ran the desk in the small Oldford branch of the society was the same age as the young policewoman; both were in their early twenties. She had none of George Taylor's old-fashioned reservations about discussing the accounts of a dead customer. Indeed, the discovery that she had a murder victim among her customers brought its own grisly glamour to her generally dull working life. She pored over the figures on the computer sheets with WPC Jane Wiseman and volunteered her own knowledge eagerly.

"I remember him well now. Good-looking chap, late thirties. Quite dishy, really, but a bit old for us. He came in regularly with cash to deposit, about once every two or three weeks. Look, you can see the dates."

Jane could indeed. There were sizeable sums put in, with very little taken out. There was over fourteen thousand pounds in the account. She studied the figures. "Very few of these deposits are in round figures, even though the sums are large."

Unlike George Taylor, the woman at her side did not expect her to make her own deductions: she was only too anxious to help, to play her part in a murder hunt. "These were all cash deposits – that's unusual nowadays, for such large sums, except from shopkeepers and publicans. Probably he was deducting cash for himself, for his own living expenses, before he put in the money. Although the sums are irregular, they are all in pounds, with no odd pence." She ran her finger down the column, stopping at £620, £530, £745. "If you ask me, he was probably paid in round hundreds and took out whatever he needed for himself before he deposited the rest here."

WPC Wiseman took the information back to the murder room at Oldford CID, hugging it to herself like a lost pet. It might be that stiff bugger DI Rushton who had established that an important piece in the Ted Giles jigsaw was missing, but it was she who had found the piece itself.

Six

G raham Reynolds was certain of one thing. He did not want to be interviewed by the police at Oldford Comprehensive School.

The news that he had been singled out for special attention by the police would fly round classrooms already overheated by the sensational news that a popular teacher had been found murdered at Broughton's Ash churchyard. The papers had portrayed Giles as a man without enemies, a man dedicated to the advancement of young people, to accentuate the mystery of his brutal death. In response to Hook's phone call to arrange a meeting, he said briskly, "By the time kids have taken the tale back to their parents it will have grown in the telling – I'll be on the verge of arrest in half the homes round here. I've a free period at ten: I'll come into the station."

Hook knew from this reaction that Reynolds had plainly been expecting the call. Sue Giles must have rung him on the Wednesday evening to tell him of the police visit to her. Only what you would have expected, DS Hook told himself; you couldn't always have surprise on your side. Perhaps, indeed, if Reynolds was planning to hide anything, it was a good thing that he had had many hours to anticipate this meeting and develop his apprehensions about it.

When Lambert and Hook came and sat down opposite him in the interview room, Graham Reynolds certainly did not look like a man who had spent a sleepless night of anticipation. He rose automatically to greet them, his hands steady on the small, square table in the middle of the high, windowless room. "First time I've been in one of these places. I can see how they help you to get confessions out of people!" Reynolds glanced round at the bare walls with their lemon emulsion paint, up at the shadeless fluorescent light, as if studying a hospital operating theatre.

Lambert smiled, remembering that this man was a sociologist, wondering if he would feel he had to reproduce certain attitudes towards police work. He said, "Interview rooms are built at public expense to serve a purpose. They are basic because our masters don't believe in unnecessary expense, any more than they do in schools."

Reynolds gave an answering smile in response to the reference to education. He had black hair that curled tightly and plentifully against his head, and his eyes were a very dark brown. They were set in an alert, quizzical face; his skin was dark, tanned almost olive even in the middle of November. He said, "I don't suppose this will take very long, because I haven't much to tell you."

"Really? Well, you could start by telling us why it has taken you until Thursday morning to come forward, when we were in the school as early as Tuesday asking for any information available about your colleague Mr Giles."

If Reynolds was surprised by the abruptness of this, by the absence of any polite preamble, he gave no outward sign of it. "That's easily answered. I felt I knew nothing that would be useful to you."

"Even though you had worked alongside Mr Giles for five years? Even though you are apparently planning to marry the woman who was still his wife at the time of his death?"

Now Reynolds did seem taken aback, perhaps by the baldness of this, and Bert Hook wondered for a moment if he was quite as committed to marriage as Sue Giles had indicated. It was normal nowadays to find different degrees of enthusiasm for marriage in people who ac- knowledged each other readily as partners. Reynolds said evenly, "I knew no more and no less about Ted than most of his other teaching colleagues. Probably less than Mick Yates, whom I knew you had already seen on Tuesday morning at the school. As for my plans with Sue, they are irrelevant, since they had nothing to do with Ted's death."

I wonder, thought Lambert. A cool customer this, who had measured exactly what he was going to tell them when he came here and was not easily going to be teased or intimidated into more. There would have to be some verbal fencing, until an opening presented itself. He said, "Tell us all about your relationship with the late Ted Giles, then. Don't be afraid to state the obvious; bear in mind we still know very little about him."

"We taught together for five years. But there was no

overlap in our subjects; I'm Head of Social Sciences and Ted taught Chemistry and Biochemistry. We met at staff meetings, liaised a little over sixth-form studies and university applications, but our professional lives were almost entirely separate."

"And your social lives?"

"The same." Reynolds stared at the Superintendent evenly across the three feet which was all that divided them, as if challenging him to prove otherwise.

"Even though you were planning to marry his wife."

"Even though that was the situation, yes. Perhaps, indeed, because of that. It is possible to be civilised about these things, Superintendent, though I don't suppose the police come across many examples of it." Reynolds took out a packet of slim panatellas from his pocket and said, "You don't mind if I smoke?"

"On the contrary, I'd prefer that you didn't." Especially while you're being so determinedly cool and uncooperative, thought Lambert. "When was the last time you met Ted Giles outside school, Mr Reynolds?"

For a moment he looked as if he would contest the smoking refusal. Then he put the panatellas slowly back into his pocket, smiled as though he were humouring a petulant child and said, "I can't remember the last time. Probably with the rest of the staff on some end-of-term binge."

"I see. And when did you form your relationship with Mrs Giles?"

"I've known Sue for years. But I suppose we began to get serious about a year ago."

"That's when you first became lovers?"

Reynolds looked now as if he would lose his temper. The brown eyes flashed from one to the other of the men who confronted him and the arms he had kept folded flew apart. Then, with an obvious effort, he controlled himself and said, "It was, yes. Look, is all this detail really necessary?"

"Probably not. But you see, we have no real idea yet what will be useful and what won't, so we have to ask about all sorts of things. We are trying to build up a picture of a dead man, who can't tell us anything about what was important to him, what pleased him and what annoyed him. Did the fact that you were sharing his wife's bed annoy Ted Giles, Mr Reynolds?"

This time Graham Reynolds actually snorted with rage before he was able to suppress it. Then he seemed to realise that this long-faced policeman with the grizzled hair would be happy enough to rile him, to catch and store some unguarded reaction. He took a deep breath and said evenly, "No, it didn't. Ted knew his marriage was over long before Sue and I became an item. He was sensible enough to realise that."

"I see. And yet, human nature being what it is, it would not have been surprising if Mr Giles had shown resentment at your new relationship, would it? Not many people find it easy to accept another man enjoying the intimacies they once took for granted, in my experience."

Reynolds wished those unflinching grey eyes would leave his face, even for a moment. This unblinking, unembarrassed scrutiny was something he had never had to endure in his life before. He said determinedly, "There was no animosity between Ted Giles and me. I told you, we didn't meet socially, and in our professional dealings we got on perfectly well."

"I see. In that case, can you explain the fierce altercation you had with Mr Giles in his Chemistry lab on Friday the twenty-sixth of October?"

Hook, bending studiously over his notebook for most of the interview, looked up when he heard Reynolds gasp, adding the pressure of his own scrutiny to the chief's. You had to hand it to Lambert; he'd set this complacent bugger up beautifully before he played the one real card he had in his hand. Reynolds played for time, as Bert had somehow known he would. "This is Mick Yates, isn't it? Listening outside doors where he shouldn't be! Wait till I speak to that interfering young—"

"As you would expect, we cannot reveal the source of our information, Mr Reynolds. I would remind you that my team has interviewed many people at the school, including pupils. It would be as unwise of you to pursue the matter beyond this room as to utter threats within it. Meantime, I must repeat my request that you explain the source of this dispute with a man who is now dead."

It was calm, relentless; Reynolds felt he was a specimen under a microscope which had just been pronounced interesting. He found himself licking his lips, gripping the edge of the table in front of him, doing all the things he had promised himself he would not do when he came here. His voice sounded distant in his own ears as he said, "I was wrong to pretend that there was nothing between us, that our relationship was good. It wasn't. But that wasn't my doing."

Lambert permitted himself a sardonic smile, enjoying the sight of this fish wriggling upon his hook. "Come now, Mr Reynolds, you can hardly say that. Almost any man would be upset by the man who was sleeping with his wife, wouldn't he?"

"They weren't married any more. Well, they were, but in name only. Ted had ceased to have any close relationship with Sue long before I took over."

"Of course. And perhaps it wouldn't be logical for him to oppose you. But logic doesn't have a lot to do with these things, does it?"

Reynolds stared at him for a moment, as if he wished to deny the thought. Then he said sullenly, "I suppose not. It didn't in Ted's case, anyway. He wasn't quite the saint the newspaper reports of his death portray, you know. Popular teacher and man without enemies – all that stuff."

"So what were you quarrelling about on October the twenty-sixth?"

"I don't remember the details now."

Lambert let the futility of that bounce off the walls of the small, airless room. Then he said, "You can do better than that, Mr Reynolds. I'm giving you the opportunity to do so."

It sounded like a threat in Reynolds' burning ears. A threat of what? He was not sure of what, but he was no longer thinking rationally under the merciless gaze of those grey eyes. No wonder frightened adolescents signed confessions after hours in places like this. He found his mouth saying, "All right! We didn't get on as well as I said we did, Ted and I. He didn't like me taking up with

Sue. I think he hated her, would have done anything to frustrate what she wanted to do with her life."

"I see. That wasn't quite the impression Mrs Giles gave us of their relationship when we spoke to her yesterday. Perhaps we shall need to speak to her again."

This time Graham Reynolds was sure it was a threat. But he knew he mustn't offer them any more information. "Sue kept her distance from him, only spoke to him when she needed to. She didn't believe in giving him opportunities to be awkward."

"I see. Well, last Saturday night someone denied Mr Giles the right to be anything. And this morning, after pretending otherwise as long as you could, you tell me that you and he were enemies. As the man charged with investigating the murder of Edward Giles, your deceptions interest me, Mr Reynolds. I think you should now tell me what you were quarrelling about, without any further prevarication."

It was quietly spoken, but all the more insistent for that. Lambert had not raised his voice throughout the interview; even now, his tone suggested well-meant advice. And yet to Reynolds, used only to speaking to people in social situations where the conversational niceties were used to oil the wheels, he seemed inexorable. Glancing at the face of Bert Hook on Lambert's right, he found that rubicund countenance as expectant and unblinking as his questioner's, and capitulated. "We had a real row because I told him to lay off Sue. I said I was going to marry her and he said he'd put every obstacle in our way."

"But you must have known that he couldn't hold

things up indefinitely. The law is on your side, as you must be aware."

"I knew that, of course. But his attitude annoyed me. I told him as much, and we exchanged words about it, angry words. But there was no more to our quarrel than that." His mouth set in a line; the tanned, experienced features were suddenly sullen and determined as those of any child who is determined to stick to his story.

Lambert wondered if that was really all there was to the argument between the two men, but he sensed that it was all he was going to get at this stage. Reynolds was not under caution, was still officially helping the police of his own free will. Lambert said, "When did you last see Mr Giles?"

The swiftness of the switch threw Reynolds, who had been setting himself to frustrate further probing of his quarrel with Ted Giles a fortnight before his death. "I – I haven't really thought about it." That rang as false in his own ears as theirs: they all knew he must have considered the answer to this, whether he was guilty or entirely innocent. "I think I saw him in the staffroom before afternoon school last Friday afternoon. Yes, I remember now, I did. But not later than that. I was free for the last period on Friday and I left school early, you see."

Lambert ignored that. "And where were you last Saturday night, when Mr Giles was being murdered?"

The question shook most people, especially when it was framed in those blunt words. But for the first time in their exchange, Graham Reynolds smiled. He made himself take a little time, tried even to savour the moment. "I was in Ireland on Saturday night, Superintendent. Enjoying a splendid meal in a hotel in Killarney, to be precise."

Christine Lambert felt giddy as the waves of relief surged through her. For a moment she felt she might faint, falling forward from her armless chair in a heap upon the doctor's carpet. Within a few seconds, this passed, her vision cleared, and she was seized by a disconcerting urge to leap forward and embrace the grey-haired, bespectacled figure on the other side of the desk. Instead, she said simply, "You can't even guess how relieved I am. I was convinced in my own mind it was the cancer recurring, you see!"

Dr Cooper's natural caution surfaced immediately; he mustn't allow this nice middle-aged woman's relief to mislead her. When she had thought her pain stemmed from cancer, she had been adamant that he was to hold nothing back, that there was to be no room for what she had called "medical discretion" with her. He hastened now to prick her bubble of optimism before it soared out of reach. "The news may not be quite as good as you imagined, Mrs Lambert. No cancer. But a serious heart condition. We're talking about major surgery. Maybe a triple bypass."

Christine, who knew she should look grave, tried to do so and failed. "Surgery is a relief now. I thought you were going to tell me that it was cancer which had gone beyond the lymph glands, that it was simply a matter of time. I was all keyed up to refuse surgery, to refuse any treatment except painkillers, in fact. I had my speech about going swiftly and not losing dignity all ready for you."

Dr Cooper smiled. It was not often that someone greeted the necessity for a heart bypass with such elation. "There's a high chance of a successful outcome; the figures improve with each passing year. But it is a serious prospect, nonetheless, and you and your family must prepare for it properly, Christine." It was probably because of her unexpected skittishness that he used her first name. He had seen this woman through three pregnancies and breast cancer, without ever falling into that intimacy; now, with the need to impose realism upon her schoolgirl buoyancy, it had tripped out quite naturally.

It was not the serious nature of her condition but the mention of her family which brought Christine Lambert back to earth. "Yes, you're quite right, of course. I'll prepare them. One thing, though: please don't mention this to John at the moment. I'll tell him, but in my own good time."

"I'll respect your wishes, of course. But we really don't recommend keeping secrets from spouses. In the long run, it doesn't—"

"Don't worry, I'll tell him. But although he's a detective superintendent and well used to death, he can't bear any thought of it within his own family. I don't want him fussing round me like a protective mother, not until I've adjusted myself to the new situation." She wished suddenly that her own protective mother, who had been dead now these ten years, was around to see her through this. And with that thought, her levity departed and she became responsible again. "Don't worry, Doctor, I'll let him know as soon as you have a bed arranged for me.

J. M. Gregson

But John's much better at coping with thieves and murderers than with a sick wife. He rather loses balance when I'm ill. He never had to cope with it until two years ago, and I doubt whether he's a quick learner in this."

Christine prevailed, as she always did when she was determined to do so, and they left it at that. And a seriously ill woman drove home with her heart singing with hope.

Superintendent John Lambert, thought by his wife to be so good at coping with murderers, felt himself not much nearer to discovering the identity of this particular one.

He sat in his office with Chris Rushton and Bert Hook, digesting the fund of information gathered by the team, trying to isolate the five per cent of it which might be important. "Anyone at the school we should put in the frame?" he asked. "Apart from the obvious candidate, of course, who so delighted in showing us that he was in Ireland."

"That tale seems to stand up, I'm afraid," said DI Rushton, meticulous as ever, and as ever anxious to demonstrate it. "I checked the hotel in Killarney. Mr Reynolds and Mrs Giles checked in there late on Friday night. No 'Mr and Mrs John Smith' for them – I suppose hypocrisy isn't the flavour of the month now in these things, even in the Emerald Isle. They stayed until Sunday and had dinner there on Saturday night, which seems to leave both of them in the clear."

"Unless of course one of them hired a contract killer. Sue Giles certainly seems to have the money to do so, but

I doubt if she has either the contacts or the inclination to dispose of a troublesome ex-husband in that way."

"There doesn't seem to be anyone else on the staff of the school who's a likely prospect at present," said Bert Hook. "Two of the staff have had words with him in the last few years, and one or two parents have found fault with his treatment of their little darlings, but there's nothing very serious. Most people say he was a popular and successful teacher."

"We certainly haven't turned up a motive in the school for anything as serious as murder," said Rushton.

"Any clue yet as to the source of this extra income over the last two years?" said Lambert.

"Nothing. It doesn't seem to be anything educational. He didn't do A-level examining, which was my first thought. In any case, that wouldn't have raised sums like the ones involved here, and it would have come in one or two big cheques, not the fairly regular dollops of cash Giles was putting into the building society account. And he didn't do evening class teaching or work for the Open University, which might have meant monthly payments, but again not of the size he was enjoying."

"So something criminal," said Bert Hook, not without satisfaction. Large, unexplained sums often meant some activity on the wrong side of the law. And where lucrative crime was involved, violence and even murder were never very far away. This might be the most promising line of enquiry.

"No suggestion of criminal associates from anyone we've interviewed," said Rushton dolefully. "Even the rare people who didn't like Giles didn't suggest anything

very shady. But I must say he does seem to have succeeded in keeping his private life exactly that in the last
few years."

At that moment, the phone on John Lambert's desk
shrilled insistently. "Sorry to interrupt you, sir," said the
girl on the switchboard, "but I have a caller who insists
on being put through to the office in charge of the Giles
murder investigation. She won't identify herself, and I've
told her you're in conference, but—"

"Put her through, please. And put a trace on the call,"
said Lambert.

A high-pitched, female voice, discordant, near to
hysteria. "Ted Bloody Giles. Paper says he's a bloody
saint. You find out about his work with Rendezvous,
then see if you think he's such a fucking saint!"

"Please try to be calm. We—" But at the other end of
the line, the phone was crashed down.

The Rendezvous was an escort agency in Gloucester.
The trace on the call revealed only a deserted phone box.
But it looked as though they might have the source of the
late Mr Giles's extra income.

Seven

C olin Pitman was a successful businessman. Over thirty-five years, he had built up his haulage company from a one-man, one-vehicle business to a limited company which employed thirty drivers and owned sixteen heavy-duty vans and lorries. The Pitman name was familiar to the public on the sides of pantechnicons, and Colin had worked, thought and scrapped his way to a fortune. He was a rich man, proud of what he had achieved. He was also the father of Sue Giles.

A doting father, John Lambert decided, after three minutes in his company. They sat in his office, with its prints of Malvern at the turn of the century on the walls, a red leather Chesterfield which looked as if it had never been used, and a desk and swivel chair which matched the formidable bulk of the man who ran this business, which centred upon the yard outside these modest office premises. Lambert and Hook had come through that yard to meet their man. It was a busy place, with heavy goods vehicles moving carefully in and out of the service bays in the hangar-like shed where they were checked and maintained. There was a dominant smell of hot oil and diesel, which seemed to permeate even into this

room, despite the vase of golden chrysanthemums someone had set in front of the unused gas fire.

Pitman listened to the sounds outside, even as he sat
them down to talk and asked his secretary to bring
them coffee, so that they divined immediately that he
was happiest out there, with his finger on the pulse of
that invisible but scarcely soundless body he controlled. A hands-on manager this, in the modern
jargon, with firm ideas, tested in the hard commercial
world beyond the small town where he was based. A
man who was used to his own way and who did not
take kindly to argument.

He made no pretence of wondering why they had
come, though he plainly planned to offer them very
little. "It's about Ted, isn't it? Well, I'm sorry he's dead,
and I hope you catch the bugger who did for him, but I
don't see how I can be of any help to you."

A Yorkshireman, by his accent, and no doubt proud of
it and the bluntness which was supposed to accompany
the breed. Bert Hook had bowled to some eminent
cricketers but never to Boycott. He decided it must have
been rather like questioning this man: he was all dour
opposition, but ready to make you look silly if your
concentration lapsed. Lambert, responding to this attitude in the man, said without preamble, "What did you
think of your son-in-law, Mr Pitman?"

Hook, still thinking of Boycott, saw him coming down
quickly on this yorker. "Not much. Put him out of my
mind as much as I could. That's why I can't help you
now."

Lambert decided to behave as if the straight bat had

given him a chance. "Ah! You didn't much like Ted Giles, then."

Pitman looked at him suspiciously. "Course I didn't. He made my girl miserable, didn't he?" He snorted contemptuously that they should query what was so obvious and looked around him as if he wanted to spit, which he might well have done in the yard outside. He didn't dislike policemen, who had their place in the orderly world his business needed, but he preferred them in uniform; you knew where you were then, with ranks and functions. He was suspicious of anything he did not know, and he had little experience of CID men in their plain clothes.

Lambert took his time. "We know their marriage broke up. Your daughter told us it finished years ago and—"

"That's right." A little too promptly, even interrupting; perhaps an automatic response, supporting his daughter.

"And you blame Ted Giles rather than your daughter for the failure of that union?"

"Course I do. He had it made with Sue, if he'd had the sense to see it."

Lambert let the seconds stretch, but Pitman didn't enlarge upon the thought. He glared at them, breathing heavily, as if they had offered him a personal slight. Eventually Lambert said, "I'd like you to give us an account of the marriage as you saw it."

"Why should I? It's bugger all to do with you."

"In ordinary circumstances, yes. In a murder inquiry, no. You're not stupid: you will appreciate we are looking for the enemies of a man who was brutally murdered. From your attitude so far, you would appear to be one. You can't expect us not to pursue that."

Pitman glared at him, then broke into an unexpected smile. "You're a blunt man, Superintendent Lambert. In other circumstances, I might appreciate that. All right, I see your point. I didn't like Ted Giles. Not much, even from the start, though I had to make the best of it when they were getting wed. My wife were still alive then, and she saw to that." For a moment, his face clouded, and they had a glimpse of how this self-sufficient man had relied heavily upon his wife in the areas outside his work. "I don't know too much about the details of how he split with our Sue, but I do know Giles was playing away."

"He had other women?"

"That's what I said, isn't it? Whether it was one or more than one, I don't know, but she wouldn't have it. And she were right." His jaw jutted aggressively above the barrel chest, as if he was challenging them to deny him.

"Is Sue your only daughter, Mr Pitman?"

If Pitman was thrown by the sudden switch of line, he did not show it. This was a question he was often asked, and one of the few social topics he was prepared to enlarge upon. "Aye, that she is. And a good daughter, too."

"I'm sure she is. And no doubt the two of you are very close?"

He looked from one to the other of the two serious faces on the other side of the big desk, his face full of suspicion. He was saved from answering by the arrival and distribution of the coffee, but he was such a direct man that the pause did not help him. His hair was thinning and brushed straight back from his forehead, but he flicked away a non-existent curl from above his left eye in a nervous reaction that took him back forty years to the uncertain adolescent he had thought buried for ever. It was a curiously touching gesture in this big, confident bear of a man. However strong we might appear, we are all vulnerable to our children, thought Lambert. He said again, "You have a close relationship with your daughter, I think?"

"Yes. I try to look after her interests and she looks out for me. She's all I have, since my wife went. More important to me than all this." His arms rose briefly, no more than six inches in the air, but the gesture took in the whole of the industrial enterprise around him and the ultimate futility of his success.

Lambert thought of the huge house and spacious grounds where Sue Giles lived in solitary splendour. No doubt her father lived in a house that was as big or bigger than that one, not just isolated but increasingly lonely, as the prospect of retirement and old age stretched out before him. "You don't live together, though."

"No. She has her own life to lead. I see her twice a week." His terse declarations had all the determination he had shown earlier, as though two meetings a week was an arrangement he had resolved on and to which he was determined to restrict himself.

Lambert said gently, "She's told you about Graham Reynolds?"

"Of course she has. We don't have secrets."

How often the two men before him had heard parents, husbands and wives use that phrase! Sometimes people sounded as if they were trying to convince themselves, but there was no suggestion of that with Colin Pitman. Lambert said evenly, "Then you will know that she plans to marry Mr Reynolds."

"Yes. And to save you asking, I'm glad about that. He'll be all right for her, help her to make a fresh start. If he doesn't, he'll have me to answer to!"

"Just as Ted Giles did?"

Lambert spoke quietly, which only exacerbated the feeling of the furious Pitman that he had been led into a trap. He was a physical man, but there was no physical outlet for him here. He gripped the edge of his desk with both of his huge hands and said, "Clever buggers, aren't you? All right, I told Giles years ago what I thought of him, warned him that it would be the worse for him if he didn't treat Susie better."

"And how did he react?"

Pitman looked puzzled by the question, as if he had scarcely considered the detail of his enemy's response. No doubt his own anger and his own compulsion to express it had been more important than Giles's reactions. Then, as if loth to allow any credit at all to the dead man, he said reluctantly, "Giles said the faults weren't all on his side. That he hoped they'd still get back together. That I'd better talk to Sue."

"And how long ago was this?"

"About three years. I never spoke to him again." This time the answer was surprisingly prompt and precise.

"And where were you on Saturday night?"

"When Giles died, you mean? You can't come here accusing me of—"

"I can ask you where you were, Mr Pitman. You are one of the few people we have seen so far who admits to being an enemy of a man who was brutally killed. It's part of our job to know where you were when he died."

Colin Pitman looked from one face to the other, at the grey eyes of Lambert, at the pen of Hook poised expectantly over his notebook. Leaning forward, with his hands still clasping the edge of the big desk, he looked like a caged bear. "I was at home last Saturday night. The whole of it."

"I see. And no doubt you live alone."

"Yes. The woman who cleans for me doesn't operate on Saturday night." It was a rare attempt at sarcasm from this direct man; it fell awkwardly into the quiet room.

Lambert ignored it. "You stayed in the house for the whole of the evening?"

"Yes. And I've no witnesses."

Lambert smiled grimly. "We tend to suspect alibis that come neatly parcelled for us. Nevertheless, if you think of anyone who can verify your whereabouts on that evening, I'd be grateful if you'd pass on the information. To eliminate you from our enquiries, you understand."

Hook watched Pitman as Lambert reversed his old Vauxhall and drove carefully out of the busy yard. He was back among his men, directing them with his broad arms and his harsh, no-nonsense voice, back in a world he understood and dominated. They could see the relief in every movement of those strong arms.

What they did not see was that he was conscious of their every movement, even whilst apparently immersed in the operation of his business. Three minutes after they had gone, Colin Pitman was back in the privacy of his inner office, reviewing the visit, reliving the CID questions and his own responses. The outcome seemed to him satisfactory, as far as it went. These were shrewd men, more at home with murder than he could ever be.

But he didn't see how they could possibly find out where he had really been on that fateful Saturday night.

DI Rushton found himself squirming, as he had feared he might when they got round to this subject.

"Bit tricky, this Rendezvous business," said Lambert, po-faced as a Dickensian clergyman.

"Very tricky," agreed Hook, as usual catching his chief's drift immediately. "What would really be most useful would be to put an undercover man in there."

"Yes. Test the waters. Find out just how bona fide an organisation it is."

"Test whether it's just an escort agency or something more sinister."

Their faces turned in unison, innocent but speculative, to gaze at Chris Rushton. "Take a single bloke to convince them," mused Lambert.

"Preferably a good-looking younger officer, who would excite plenty of interest among their female clientele," said Hook.

"But a responsible senior man, who wouldn't land

himself in any embarrassing situations. There must be someone around here who could do it. Someone who might even enjoy doing it." He pursed his lips, without removing his eyes from Rushton.

"Wonderful chance for the right man. Free crumpet at public expense. Free *desperate* crumpet, I shouldn't wonder." Hook whistled quietly at the thought.

Rushton found his voice at last. The awful vision of the night when he had gone undercover in a situation like this, ending up drunk and with his trousers over his arm on a Cheltenham street at midnight, swam before him, removing all power of speech by its nightmare vividness. Eventually he blurted, "Not me! Definitely not me, if that's what you're thinking, sir. I couldn't do it. I just couldn't!" Like many humourless men, he was often unsure whether those around him were serious or not.

Lambert looked incredulous. "You thought you might be the man for the job, Chris? Well, I'd never even entertained the thought, but now that you suggest it . . ." He looked speculatively at his co-conspirator.

Hook was on cue with his enthusiasm. "My word, yes! Right under our noses, and we didn't see it! Ideal man for the job. Young, good-looking, without serious ties. He'd be a natural!" The two faces turned back to Chris Rushton, managing the difficult feat of looking at the same time both bland and expectant.

"No way!" said Rushton. "I'm quite ready to admit I don't have the skills for undercover work. Not this kind, anyway."

Lambert allowed his face to fall, not all at once, but in a staircase of disappontments, until all was gloom on the long, lined visage. "Pity, that. We could have gleaned all kinds of useful information. Feather in the cap of the man who secured it, obviously."

"Accelerated promotion, I shouldn't wonder," mused Hook. Even his cheerful features descended into despondency at the thought of this opportunity forsaken.

Lambert decided they had allowed themselves enough light relief. "Perhaps we'll just have to go round there ourselves. Confront them directly, if we've no one up to the deceptions needed."

"Muddle our way through as usual," agreed Hook dolefully.

And the two grizzled veterans turned away to the meeting they had always planned, leaving behind them a handsome young inspector who had been stripped of all his usual confidence.

Christine Lambert was preoccupied with much more serious matters. Her daughter Caroline was giving her advice she did not want to hear.

"You'll have to tell Dad, you know," she said. "And quickly. You should have told him already, before me and Jacky."

"He's busy with his own concerns. He's got quite enough on his plate – he's in charge of the investigation of that schoolteacher's murder."

"You used to complain about that in the old days, when we were kids. Said he shut you out of his life for his job. Now you're trying to shut him out."

She was right on both counts, thought Christine. How much children knew, when you thought you were concealing things! And how little they said! She had thought in those dark years when she and John had almost split up because of his intense involvement in his work that their late-night quarrels had escaped the sleeping girls. Now the humorous, alert blue eyes which stared so steadily into her own seemed more adult, more knowledgeable about life, than she felt herself. She added another lame cliché to those she had offered already to her daughter. "I – I'm still coming to terms with it myself, you see."

Caroline smiled at the worried, ageing face she knew so well. "Tell him, Mum. Tell him you thought it was the cancer back again, that you thought it was the end. Tell him that a heart bypass operation is a relief, not a blow. But tell him quickly. Don't let him think he's been kept in the dark, while Jacky and I knew all about it."

"All right. Let me choose my moment, that's all."

"Of course. Just so long as that isn't an excuse for more delay."

"No. I'll tell him in the next few days, I promise."

"In the next twenty-four hours. It's not fair to us to expect us to keep the secret."

"All right. By tomorrow night, then."

"Right. And don't build up the problem for yourself in anticipation. He's a good listener, Dad is. And good in a crisis."

It was true; Christine Lambert knew it was. But it gave her an unexpected comfort to hear her daughter saying it. She grinned at the younger woman, as they sat in their armchairs with their cups of tea almost forgotten at their sides. "You didn't always think that when you were battling with him in your teenage days!"

"I did really, you know, even though I wouldn't always acknowledge it. And Jacky and I never doubted he loved us, however much he ranted at us. And he loves you, Mum. He'll be very hurt if he thinks you've kept things from him."

"All right, it's agreed. Don't go on at a sick woman!" Christine stood up and ruffled her daughter's soft brown hair, as she had been used to do when she was a young girl. Where had those twenty years gone so quickly? Another cliché, but nonetheless true for that, Christine Lambert thought, as she prepared to face a future which suddenly seemed quite brief.

On the other side of Oldford, another daughter was reassuring another parent. "We'll be okay, Dad, I told you. Whoever killed Ted, they can't possibly suspect me. Or Graham. We were in Ireland at the time. And you were at home all that night. If you'd had a convenient witness to that, it would have looked quite suspicious – a departure from your normal routine. The police are going through the motions. It's routine procedure."

Colin Pitman knew it was true really, that he could have worked all that out for himself without ringing his daughter. "It's just that they seemed to be looking right through me. To know so much more already than I did."

"I know. They gave me the same feeling when they came here. I expect it's an impression they always try to create."

"Yes. They did say they had a lot of other people to see."

"And they will have. Ted had all kinds of contacts in

these last few years. Trust me, they'll be much more interested in them than in my old dad."

"I expect you're right. And not so much of the old, young lady!" He tried to summon his usual warmth, but it rang hollow in his own ears. He wished she was there in front of him, warm and convincing, instead of invisible at the other end of the phone line.

"See you soon, then, Dad." She rang off before he could pin her down to a time. She did not want to confront that caring, anxious face for a few days yet.

Eight

G loucester is a compact city. The town grew up around the ancient cathedral, and the medieval cross formed by the thoroughfares of Eastgate, Westgate, Northgate and Southgate still dominates the central shopping area. The modern commercial citadels of Sainsbury's, B & Q and their rivals sprawl far outside the environs of the old town beside the Severn, but most people still think of Gloucester as the area within the line of the old city walls.

People seeking to establish small businesses look for premises in this central area: the worshippers of God and Mammon come together in a way which would have been comfortable enough for those crafty medieval friars who built the cathedral around the bones of the assassinated King Edward II, knowing it would bring interested pilgrims to them.

So the headquarters of the introduction agency Rendezvous stood, incongrously to modern eyes, within the long winter shadow of the massive stone walls of the cathedral which had dominated the area for six centuries. But there was no winter sun on the bleak afternoon of the 16th of November, when Lambert and Hook visited the place. The rain slanted down from cloud which was so low that it seemed already night, though it was no more than three thirty. Though they knew well enough of the place's existence, neither man had been here before. But there was no difficulty in finding it: the letters of Rendezvous in garish green neon lighting blazed out brazenly from the gloom.

The young woman who came forward assumed they were prospective clients and turned upon them her most encouraging smile. "Do come in and sit down!" she said, as if they were lingering diffidently in the doorway, instead of standing already within a yard of her neat desk. She went straight into her standard opening spiel. "There's no need to be shy. You'd be surprised how many busy people find that their social lives are a little – undeveloped. That's what we're here for and—"

"We're not customers," said Lambert, hastily flashing a warrant card before the girl could get any deeper into her routine patter. "Detective Sergeant Hook and I are here on police business – rather serious business, as a matter of fact."

As the girl's jaw dropped, the door behind her desk opened and an older woman appeared. She had dark blue eyes beneath yellow hair, which might or might not have been naturally blonde, for there was no hint of darkness at the roots. The hair was a little too tightly and regularly curled for contemporary tastes, and the eyes assessed them shrewdly, recognising them immediately as plainclothes policemen, as the girl in front of her had not. "I think you'd better come through to my office," the woman said.

She wore a dark green suit and leather shoes which exactly matched it. The jacket fell open as she sat down and revealed a lambswool sweater that clung tight over the well-supported breasts beneath it. "Pat Roberts," she said after Lambert had given her their names. They did not shake hands. Her eyes studied them unhurriedly, trying to assess the seriousness of their visit from her point of view. Just when they thought they would have to make the first move, she said, "We run a business that is perfectly above board, Superintendent. There are a lot of lonely people in the world today. We introduce some of them to each other."

Lambert smiled. "Yes. It says so in your brochure. It also indicates your price for doing so. It must be a profitable enterprise."

Pat Roberts smiled back, but there was no humour in her face. Despite her careful make-up, they saw now that she was older than she had appeared at first: probably around fifty. "We provide more than introductions. We try to match like with like. And if at first they don't succeed, we enable them to try and try again." There was just a suggestion of contempt for the clients who brought the profits, but the implication was that she could afford to be candid with policemen, who saw life for what it was.

Lambert saw a hard woman, a woman who would be not just clear-sighted but ruthless whenever she felt it was necessary. No doubt most of the clients of the agency, encouraged along by those bright young faces at the reception desks in the outer office, never met this woman. He said, "I think you know why we're here, Ms Roberts. We are interested in one of your customers."

"Edward Giles?"

"You did know."

"I guessed correctly. I read my papers. And I know it must be serious, to bring the top brass in here."

"So why did you not come to us? There's been an appeal out, for four days now. No doubt you read that as well."

"Our files are confidential. It's one of the things our customers expect; one of the reasons they pay the fees you just said were so extravagant."

"I see. Well, you will be aware that this is a murder inquiry, so that your normal rules of confidentiality will be waived."

She shrugged. "You can look at Edward Giles's file, if you like. It's sparse and uninteresting. He joined us just over two years ago. He hasn't been back since a couple of early meetings. We never take the initiative in contacting our clients: we assume that we have met their requirements and are well satisfied with our service if they do not continue to use the facilities for which they enrolled."

"Fair enough. And lucrative enough, no doubt, when people pay a hefty year's subscription in advance and then don't bother you. I have no doubt you have a thin, blameless file on Ted Giles, possibly compiled in the last few days with this very meeting in mind. That is of no interest to us."

She looked for a moment as if she would respond to the insult with interest. Then she said coldly, "Then I don't think we can be of any further service to you."

"Oh, but you can. Of course, if you don't choose to cooperate, we may need to investigate the business behind the business. The services beyond the ones detailed in your attractive brochure."

"I don't know what you mean. We're a bona fide agency."

"Really?" Lambert regarded her steadily for a few seconds, then tired of this preliminary fencing. "Tell me, would you be the same Patricia Rawlings who went down for living off immoral earnings in Stafford seven years ago?"

She looked furiously from Lambert's calm, unblinking stare to the more weatherbeaten face beside him. "The name is a little different, but the face looks remarkably similar," said Hook equably. "A triumph of the modern cosmetic art, Pat."

"You bastards were just playing with me!" She hissed her resentment, but there was nevertheless an air of resignation about her.

"We did our homework before we came, that's all," said Lambert.

"I served my time for that. You can't—"

"You served a little time, it's true. The probationary period could still be invoked, of course, if you were a naughty girl, and fell back into your old ways."

"And you're saying I have."

"Let's just say I don't think you'd have got the job of managing this place with your record. Not if putting innocent singles in touch with each other was all that was involved."

Hook added his professional smile to his chief's. "Once a whore, always a whore, they tend to say in the police. Terrible cynics, most of them."

"Of course, the more intelligent ones tend to give up the game as they become veterans and manage the younger ones. Bit like football, really," said Lambert.

She was furious, yearning to fling herself like a spitting tiger on that long, complacent face, to scratch out those grey eyes which studied her so relentlessly. But she had more sense than that. She knew these men held every card that mattered. Eventually she said through gritted teeth, "What is it you want from me?"

"Perhaps just some information, provided you are completely frank with us."

She thought quickly. If they knew as much as they obviously did, and hadn't moved in, it might just be that they meant what they said. Some police forces were prepared to let her kind of enterprise go, if it was well managed and discreet and not attached to a drugs empire. She said, "What information?"

"Ted Giles. What he was really doing at Rendezvous, not what you were trying to fob us off with five minutes ago."

She reached up and patted the curls of yellow hair, as if to reassure herself; giving information to the filth did not come easily to her. "All right. He didn't come to us. We approached him. We – we run an escort service as well as the meetings agency. Edward Giles – he was always known as that to us, because the full name goes down better with the kind of ladies who pay for an escort – was on our list of unattached men who were available to squire ladies who could afford it."

"And no doubt his services sometimes went beyond merely escorting them for an evening out."

"That is nothing to do with us. We provide an escort agency. If relationships develop from it, that is the business of the people concerned, not us."

It was the standard reply. But people like Pat Roberts, née Rawlings, knew which people wanted merely a partner for an evening at the theatre and which women were in search of sex and prepared to pay for it. And which men also, of course: that was an even more lucrative avenue. He grinned at the hard face of the woman who glared her hostility across her desk. "I might even buy that, if you give us a full and frank account of Ted Giles. I might tell you that we know what you were paying him. We can produce the bank statements – in court, if we need to."

"We paid Edward Giles to provide an escort service. You can't prove otherwise."

Lambert sighed. "We may not need to, if you cooperate fully. At the moment, I'm only interested in who killed Ted Giles. We need a list of the women you paid him to see. And your views on which if any he was seeing frequently – for whatever reason."

Pat Roberts stared at him for a moment, as if she was weighing the possibilities of deceit. Then she said, "Fair enough. I'll give you the names."

"That would be sensible. And don't forget you're helping the police with their enquiries. Ignore anyone Giles saw only once or twice two years ago, at the beginning of his time with you. The person who's likely to interest us is someone he saw frequently, in the last few months."

"All right, I get the picture. I'll tell you who Edward

was seeing." She permitted herself her first smile in several minutes. "There are five or six of them, though; it will be up to you to work out which ones are important." That thought seemed to give Ms Roberts a lot of satisfaction.

John Lambert was late home that Friday night. The business of tracing the women from Rendezvous had been set in motion. The house-to-house check had now revealed that three different people in the village of Broughton's Ash thought they had seen a white van on the lanes there on the previous Saturday evening. Two of them had been going to and from the village inn, but the third had been walking his dog in the autumn darkness when he had had to take hasty evasive action to avoid the vehicle leaving the village. All three witnesses were vague about time and model, but they did not contradict each other. If the van had been involved at all in the conveying of Giles's body to Broughton's Ash, it had done so between eleven and midnight.

Lambert, who had consumed nothing substantial for eight hours, now found himself too tired to eat. Then he fell asleep in front of the television set, as his wife had known he would. It was not until he was clasping his mug of tea at eleven o'clock that Christine Lambert could fulfil her promise to her daughter. "I went to the doctor's yesterday."

The man who had recently been so drowsy was instantly alert. "I said you'd been looking tired. What did old Cooper have to say?"

Christine poured it all out at once, not daring to draw

back once she started, anxious to have it over and done with and her promise to Caroline honoured. "He had the results of the tests and X-rays the hospital took last week. I didn't tell you about those at the time because I didn't want you worrying unnecessarily. It's a heart problem. I'm going to need a bypass operation. But Dr Cooper says we're not to worry, because the techniques and the technology have advanced so much in the last ten years that it's now a routine operation and—"

She found herself in his arms, her face against his chest and further explanations impossible. He held her hard, this undemonstrative man she now felt she still did not know after thirty years. She felt him kneading her shoulder blades, then stroking the back of her neck under her hair, as he had been used to do before they were married when he soothed away some real or imagined trouble. It seemed a long time before he held her away from him, still with his hands on her shoulders. His grey eyes looked down into her blue ones and he said softly, "You should have told me, you know, Chris."

It was years since he had used that form of her name. Her parents, who had thought that girls should be girls and there should be no confusion about the matter, had always insisted upon the full form of her name. He had used "Chris" only when they were alone during their courtship, making it their own ridiculous secret. She remembered how he had used it when he first saw her after the birth of each of their daughters, and on the awful day when the eldest of them had died in infancy. But she had always been Christine to him in front of the children, her parents' wishes preserved into the next

97

generation. She said lamely, "Yes, I should have told you. But you are an old worrier, you know, where I'm concerned."

"Or the children."

"Yes. Or the grandchildren, now, I expect." She reached up and ran her small fingers through his grizzled, still plentiful hair.

He held her a little further away from him, staring into her face as if he was anxious to register its every nuance of expression. "You're quite sure that that's all it is? The heart?"

Despite herself, she burst out laughing. "Not many people would regard a heart bypass as trivial." She stopped laughing as suddenly as she had begun as she saw the fear in his face. "You thought it was the cancer coming back, didn't you?"

"Yes. I was worried when you seemed to tire so easily. It's not like you, and—"

"You're right. I should have told you everything that was going on at the time, the tests and so forth. I thought I was shielding you. But you were worrying the cancer was coming back, just like me." Her hand strayed instinctively to her side, crept upwards towards the breast she had had removed a year earlier. "You're quite a perceptive old thing, really, Jack Lambert!" And this time, as she used the diminutive of his name that his mother had always forbidden, it was she who put her arms round him and fell against that comfortable chest.

"It's my job to be." She felt the chest tremble a little with mirth. "But you always told me I hadn't to bring the job home with me."

When they made love twenty minutes later, she had to tell him that he need not be quite so careful of her heart, and they dissolved into giggles together at this crucial moment. It was not until they were lying on their backs in the darkness some time later that Christine said, "Perhaps if we both live to be ninety we shall become quite a well-adjusted couple."

Nine

There was one woman among the list given to them by Pat Roberts who looked promising.

Bert Hook looked at the sheet of paper with the small coloured photograph in the top right-hand corner. "Constance Elson. Reading between the lines of this, she's forty-six, separated, rich and desperate for sex. Looks like we should send Chris Rushton."

Lambert grinned. "It's tempting. But perhaps too cruel – and certainly too important. I think I'll send Bert Hook."

"Not on his own you won't!" said Bert. "I don't want promotion. But I do want to survive."

It was a bit of cheerful male chauvinism they would not have been brave enough to indulge in if there had been female ears pricked to hear, but there were not many people in the CID section on Saturday morning, even in the Murder Room, which was now crowded with material gathered in the Edward Giles case. In the end, as they had known they would, Lambert and Hook went to visit the lady together. "Safety in numbers," said Hook. Lambert had hoped an Open University literature course might have helped him to avoid such clichés.

101

But Constance Elson turned out to be something of a cliché lady, in appearance at least. She lived in a bungalow with a garden which, even in the second half of November, looked tidy enough to be in *Homes and Gardens*. There was not a weed to be seen in the long, neat borders; in one, wallflowers had recently replaced annuals, in a second, roses made a determined late flowering above a carpet of mulching bark, in a third, dahlias, which any night now would be cut down by the frost which had so far spared them, threw gaudy splashes of colour defiantly into the grey day. Yet Bert Hook knew as soon as he saw the lady who opened the door to them that she had never soiled a finger to achieve this.

"I am indeed Constance Elson," she said huskily, extending a warm, immaculately manicured hand to each of them in turn. "But please call me Connie. And do come inside! I've got the coffee ready. I'm sure you could use a cup." She turned an elegant back confidently upon them and led the way into an expensively but rather floridly furnished lounge. "Please be seated!" she said, waving her arm expansively at two sofas and three armchairs. Even at this hour on a Saturday morning, she wore high heels and an haute couture dress which was perhaps one size too small for her, so that her bottom waggled in compulsive animation within two feet of Hook's nose as she turned to the kitchen.

He caught John Lambert's eye as they stared after her beneath the twin chandeliers of the big room. She had left the door open; neither of them dared to voice a thought during the two minutes of her absence. She brought in a large tray, with a plate of flapjacks and chocolate biscuits as well as a pot of coffee, then sat in a low chair opposite them and crossed her nyloned legs. Hook, lifting his china cup carefully and sitting opposite her, decided this was certainly a change for the better from visiting and interrogating people like Aubrey Bass, Ted Giles's egregious neighbour.

"I can't imagine what I can have to say which will be of any interest to important people like superintendents," she said, turning what she considered her most winning smile upon Lambert. That was interesting, he thought. She must have known why they wanted to see her, must surely have expected to be contacted from the moment she knew that Ted Giles was dead. It set him wondering about exactly how much she knew about that death. "Hell hath no fury . . ." was another cliché, but one they saw illustrated often enough in their investigations into violent crimes.

"You will be aware, I'm sure, of the murder of Ted Giles a week ago. It is my responsibility to find out who killed him."

"I see."

"As you would expect, we are contacting everyone who knew Mr Giles well. Especially anyone who had regular contact with Mr Giles in the months before his death."

"And I am one of those people! Well, this is really rather exciting! Am I a suspect in a murder case?"

Lambert smiled into the wide-eyed, expectant face. She was like an amateur actress simulating girlish innocence. She was a little old in the tooth for the part. "We need to eliminate you from our enquiries. We also need to find out things about Mr Giles from you."

"What kind of things?"

"Things about his way of life. About where he went and what he knew. About people who might have had some wish to see him dead."

"I don't know anyone who would have wanted to harm Ted. He was a lovely man." She had seemed until now like someone guying herself, like a consciously overstated and slightly comic version of the femme fatale. Her assertion about the dead man was a standard line, yet with it the brittle pretence dropped away and she seemed both serious and accessible. Love, whatever its nature, however unlikely or ridiculous it might seem to outsiders, could leave anyone vulnerable.

Lambert said, "I'm glad you liked him. And, needless to say, we're sorry he's dead. We know a lot more about him now than we did at the beginning of the week. But what people felt about him is the most difficult thing for us to unearth. You thought he was a lovely man, and you saw a lot more of him than most people."

"I saw him pretty regularly, in the last months of his life." She looked for a moment as if she would weep, then bit her lip and forced her voice to right itself. "I first met him back in May. I am a patron of the Welsh National Opera. They sent me tickets for a gala performance of *Rigoletto* in Cardiff. I didn't want to appear there unaccompanied. I phoned Rendezvous and hired an escort."

It is surprising how much of our lives we can reveal to perceptive listeners. They knew in that moment that she had used the agency before, that she was a lonely woman. But they did not pursue these other contacts; as yet, there was no need to open up windows into the lives of men who had sold who knew what services. Lambert prompted gently, "So you wanted someone to accompany you to a prestige social occasion. Someone presentable in those circles, no doubt. But you say you didn't know Mr Giles at all before last May?"

"No. I was just relieved to find someone so suitable for the occasion. Someone who looked good in evening dress and could hold a conversation about opera was all I asked for. Edward was all of that and more. I liked him from the first and I think he liked me. That's one of the problems, you see, divining what your partner for the evening really thinks of you. When you pay for an acceptable escort, he pretends to be enjoying himself, if he's good at the role, but you often don't really know whether he likes your company. Not on a first outing."

"I suppose not. But you say you saw a lot more of Mr Giles in the months which followed."

"Yes. We eventually became very close." She could not keep the pride out of her voice.

"How often did you see him?"

"After that first time, I left it about a fortnight. Then I rang Rendezvous and booked him again. By the end of August, we were meeting every week, usually on a Friday night. In the last two months, we must have averaged twice a week."

"Thank you. That's very helpful. And you obviously feel that Mr Giles returned your feelings."

"I don't feel, Mr Lambert, I know. Edward was a bit

guarded at first, and I know I'm a little older than him – five years, if you really want to know – but he wanted to be with me."

"Permanently?"

"Yes. We'd discussed it, but agreed there was no need to rush things. He'd had an unhappy marriage and been hurt by it. He had certain objections to divorce – he was born a Catholic, you know – but they weren't insuperable."

Lambert had the familiar regret that the dead man could not be here to answer for himself. The facts argued certain reservations on his part that Connie Elson was not confronting. Both of them were unattached. There was no reason why they should not have met more than once or twice a week. Had Giles been less willing to take this further than she supposed? Had he, at worst, been a man on the make with a rich divorcee, anxious for whatever he could take from the liaison without serious commitment to it? That might mean just easy sex, or more material things like money or presents. On the other hand, he might indeed have been as committed as she claimed, cautiously increasing his meetings with her as his damaged confidence and his attachment increased. From what they had learned of him in the school and elsewhere, Giles hadn't seemed a diffident man, but men confident in a more public context could be uncertain in the more intimate world of the emotions. The difficulty with this sort of problem was that it was difficult to find third parties who had watched from the sidelines and could offer detached opinions on the degree of the man's commitment.

Hook said, "We need to know where you were on the night of Saturday the tenth of November, Mrs Elson."

"When Ted was killed, you mean? You want to know where I was when poor Ted was murdered?" There was a suggestion of hysteria to her voice now, but there were few people more fitted to calm a woman on edge than the stolid Bert Hook.

"For elimination purposes. That is how we work, you see." He flicked over a page of his notebook.

"Yes. Yes, of course I realise that. It's just – just that I've never been involved in anything like this before, you see. Well, I was here, as it happens. Watched a little television. Had quite an early night, as a matter of fact. Read for an hour or so in bed." She was brittle, nervous in her delivery, as if she realised that it sounded a thin story.

"And was anyone with you during the evening?"

"No. No, I don't think there was. I suppose that's a nuisance, isn't it?"

Hook didn't reply. It was Lambert who said, "It's a nuisance for all of us, Mrs Elson, but no more than that. If you should think of anyone who could verify that you were here – someone who rang you and spoke to you during the evening, for instance – please let us know. When did you last see Edward Giles?"

He thought perhaps the abruptness of his question had shocked her. She looked disconcerted, even embarrassed for a good ten seconds. Then she said, "He was here on that Saturday afternoon. For three and a quarter hours." The precision spoke more of her involvement with him than any declaration she had made. "We talked about

107

our plans. And – and we went in there and made love."
She gestured towards the hall and her bedroom beyond
it. "Ted had to go out in the evening, you see. He had a
commitment with someone from the school."

It was the first they had heard of that. Lambert was
pretty sure from his team's enquiries around the staff of
Oldford Comprehensive that Giles had had no such
meeting arranged. As he had expected, Constance Elson
could give him no further details of anyone involved. He
said, "What time did Mr Giles leave here?"

"At quarter to six. I wanted him to stay for a meal, but
he said he was running late."

They would have to find where Giles had really gone
on that Saturday night. Or had been intending to go:
perhaps he had never got there.

They did have one set of facts, however, which were
suggestive in themselves. They had the details of Ted
Giles's steady income from Rendezvous. Lambert, forcing himself to voice the name she had urged them to use,
said, "Forgive me, Connie, but I must ask this. Did you
go on paying Rendezvous to arrange your meetings with
Mr Giles?"

Her face flushed and a jewelled hand flashed as it was
lifted towards it. For a moment, he thought she would
blaze out at him in temper. Then she dropped her fierce
brown eyes to the carpet and said with forced control,
"No. I paid for only three meetings: the first expedition
to Cardiff and two more. After that, Edward said he
enjoyed seeing me and we met as friends. We became
lovers after about a month."

Clearly it was all documented in her mind. The

important thing from their point of view was that the payments from Rendezvous into Giles's account at the Halifax had gone on until the time of his death. He had been seeing other women and been paid for his attentions. Had Connie Elson found out about this and been furious? Or had some other woman found out about her?

While Bert Hook was enjoying Connie Elson's flapjacks, Aubrey Bass was tidying his flat.

His efforts would certainly not have met the exacting standards Ms Elson demanded from her staff. He ran the aged vacuum sketchily over those areas of the carpet that were not covered by furniture or discarded newspapers, gathered up four empty beer cans from beside his usual armchair, washed the saucepans which had accumulated over the last few days, and straightened the blankets and sheets on his bed.

Aubrey looked round the place without much satisfaction after his efforts and sighed heavily. Even to his biased eye, the flat didn't look much like home. Women had their uses, however much of a nuisance they could be at times. But perhaps now he'd finished his labours he should change his shirt. He went and peered unenthusiastically at the drably coloured garments crumpled together in his washing basket beside the washer. Clean, these were: funny how the colours ran in the hot water – someone should warn people about that. He spied a once-white T-shirt which was now grey with a tinge of blue and pulled it over his head; Aubrey didn't believe in ironing. The multiple creases eased themselves away as they stretched over his ample stomach, until the legend *Fulham for the Cup* again became legible.

Curious how a clean shirt made you itch, thought Aubrey. Perhaps it was something in the washing powder. He crossed his hands over his chest, scratched himself vigorously under both arms, turned to the racing page of the *Sun*, and sat down with his pencil. You couldn't put off the serious work of the day for ever.

He had got no further than the three thirty at the first meeting when there was an insistent knocking at his door. Aubrey always ignored the first two attempts to disturb him: unless he was expecting someone specific, it was a principle of his to do so. When the third round of knocking proved even more prolonged and insistent, he sighed, muttered a curse, and went to the door.

It was the police, for the second time in four days. This time two youngish men in uniforms stood on the landing. "Bloody 'ell," said Aubrey Bass sourly. "Can't a man even enjoy 'is weekends in peace now?"

The uniforms even knew his nickname. "Morning, Alfie," said the elder constable. He pushed the door, widening the gap from the few reluctant inches Bass had accorded him, and strolled into the flat. His younger, fresh-faced colleague followed him, unconsciously imitating his movements. They looked with distaste round the living room Aubrey thought he had cleaned. "Enjoying your Saturday after a hard week's work, were you? Well, we have to disrupt your well-earned rest, I'm afraid. Our instructions are to take you down to the station, you see. You've strayed a bit out of your depth this time, Alfie. It's in connection with a homicide last Saturday night, I believe."

By three o'clock on that November afternoon, the morning sun which had lit up the dahlias in Connie Elson's garden was long gone. Low cloud had settled heavily over the Oldford golf course and no birds sang, save for the occasional discordant cawing of an invisible rook.

To Bert Hook, it mattered not a jot. In his heart, the sun filtered its brilliant gold through the tops of the trees, a million small birds sang their intricate harmonies, and he walked through a Garden of Eden. For he was beating John Lambert at golf. He walked very softly on his large policeman's feet, as if he feared that any careless footfall might shatter the eggshell of his lead.

It was Lambert who had suggested the foray into this fantasy world. "It will clear our minds," he explained to a Hook who pretended reluctance. "We can't do anything more at the moment. We'll go into the Murder Room later and see if anything's turned up. After all, it is Saturday!" And with this conclusive British thought, he had turned the car away from the Oldford Police Station, back past Connie Elson's opulent bungalow and into the green acres of the golf club.

At two o'clock the first tee had been deserted, since all the four-balls intending to play eighteen holes had been off by one o'clock to beat the early twilight. "We should get thirteen in," Lambert had said, once again affording his sergeant the benefit of his years of experience in the ancient game. He did not know that Bert Hook had been practising with plastic aeroflight balls on the back lawn

111

of his garden, dedicating his few spare daylight moments to this game he affected to despise.

Now that self-sacrifice was paying off, and Bert was determined that they should play the full eighteen holes. He hurried between his shots, waited impatiently while his chief, who was by no means a slow player, took what seemed to Bert an age over each stroke. On a deserted course, they had completed eight holes rapidly and he was two up. Off the course, there was no greater admirer of John Lambert than this man who had been his detective sergeant and acolyte for ten years. Here, in this eerily quiet theatre of war between the tall oaks, he was determined to thrash the pompous bastard out of sight.

Lambert eventually dispatched his ball with the 5-iron over which he had fidgeted for so long. It cleared the greenside bunker by a foot, bounced off the back of it, and ran across the green towards the flag. "Judged that rather well," said John Lambert, with what he imagined was becoming modesty.

"Jammy bugger!" growled Bert Hook, with infinitely greater feeling.

Lambert just missed his three; his putt lipped the hole before finishing two feet past it. He looked expectantly at Hook, waiting for the formality of a concession, and found his sergeant staring ostentatiously at the autumn colour of a beech tree. Lambert shrugged tolerantly, smiled at the pettiness of his opponent, and nonchalantly addressed this tiddler. Too nonchalantly, perhaps. The ball lipped the hole and stayed obstinately on the edge. "That's a half, then!" snapped Hook, almost before the ball had ceased to move. He was away to the next tee at a

112

brisk military medium, so that Lambert's reaction was wasted upon a broad and oblivious back.

Lambert was still two down after the thirteen holes he had suggested, whereupon he proposed that they should stop at that point. "It's what we agreed," he said mildly.

"No, it isn't!" said his opponent vehemently. "It's what *you* agreed. I never agreed to it." He stopped for a moment, puzzled by the semantics of this: could one man on his own agree anything? Then he said, "Anyway, there's plenty of light yet!" and strode conclusively towards the fourteenth tee.

In truth, the darkness was settling fast. When they reached the sixteenth, the ridge of the Malvern Hills which was usually so appealing from the tee was completely invisible. There was no way they would be able to complete eighteen holes. But Bert Hook had seen a way to make eighteen unnecessary. If he could get three holes ahead by the end of the sixteenth, he would have won. He was still two up, and he now produced a bright yellow ball which would be more easily spotted. He dispatched it into the gloom below them from the elevated tee. Lambert affected not to see it, which his opponent thought thoroughly unsporting. But it was straight, and they found it on the fairway, five yards behind Lambert's grubby white ball.

Peering fiercely at the back of his ball in the gloom, Hook dispatched it towards the green, having instructed his companion to watch it closely this time. "You thinned the bugger!" Lambert informed him with relish.

"I thinned the bugger straight!" came the grim rejoinder.

113

With much grumbling about miners' lamps and police torches, Lambert addressed his barely visible ball with infinite care. To Hook's mind, he shuffled his feet interminably on the damp ground. But eventually he had to hit it, and when he did, his opponent had to report dutifully on the result. "High and wide," he said, trying unsuccessfully to keep the satisfaction out of his voice. "Probably in the right-hand bunker."

Hook was twenty yards ahead of Lambert by the time they reached the bottom of the slope. His bright yellow ball smiled at him from the green, no more than fourteen feet from the hole. From his right, he heard Lambert say loftily, "You were wrong, Bert. I'm not in the bunker."

"Not yet!" returned Bert, grimly and unsportingly.

It was a prophetic thought. In the near-darkness, with much muttering about the impossibility of playing any shot in these conditions, Lambert topped his ball into the sand. The Superintendent was a mild-mannered man who never swore in a working environment where there was much lurid language. He now addressed his ball as an intimate female orifice to which it bore no obvious resemblance.

Bert Hook's heart sang. Two minutes later, he holed a second putt his opponent made him take from under a foot, to secure his victory. There was no need now for the Stygian darkness of the last two holes.

It was very quiet in the car on the way back to Oldford.

Aubrey Bass had now been helping the police with their enquiries for six hours. He was certain that was what he was doing, because every time he embarked on one of his ritual grumbles they told him so.

For five of those hours, he had sat in a cell. He had muttered about wrongful arrest, but without any great conviction, because he knew he was responsible for so many things which could lead to rightful arrest. And he talked occasionally to the Station Sergeant about bringing in a brief, but his words were always attached to a nasal moan asserting, "I ain't done nothing and you can't fit me up with nothing." In view of this constant assertion of his innocence, it didn't seem to him natural to demand legal assistance. Let them come up with a proper charge, and then he'd think about it. He didn't trust lawyers anyway, and the ones you got on legal aid least of all.

When he was taken back into the interview room for a second session, he was surprised to find another odour impinging on the close and fetid atmosphere of that box of stale air. Perfume. A woman, tall and willowy in jeans and a dark blue top, with a striking oval face and long dark hair. Now in other circumstances . . . Steady, Aubrey old lad, he told himself. This was still a cop shop.

As if to reinforce that thought, Rushton, the Inspector who had grilled him when they first brought him in, now set the cassette of the tape-recorder turning, and told it that Detective Sergeant Ruth David was to be present with them at this interview. DS David sat down behind Rushton, in a corner of the small room, and Aubrey dragged his eyes from her bust to the stern face of the man on the other side of the small, square table. From no more than three feet away, DI Chris Rushton was looking at him with an undisguised, wholly professional, contempt.

"Now then. You are Alfie Bass, small-time crook. Receiving and disposing of stolen goods. Break-ins and burglaries and general buggering about. Failure a speciality."

Aubrey said nothing. For once, he hadn't done much. Not recently. So let them make the running. He scratched his left shoulder with the fingers of his right hand, lowered the corners of his broad lips in disapproval as he shook his head, looked up at the corner of the ceiling to show his boredom. Let them make the running.

They did, in a way that set Aubrey's lazy heart pounding. "You own a white Escort van, registration number F829 GHR."

"You know I do. You asked me about it earlier. A lot bloody earlier, now."

"Yes. Well, we've had the forensic lads look at it, while you've been enjoying our hospitality here. Just a preliminary glance – those lads don't work as hard as us at the weekend. But it was very interesting, Alfie."

"It's Aubrey."

"All right, Aubrey. If you're moving into the serious criminal league, we might as well give you a serious name. So Aubrey Algernon Bass, if you like."

This cold sod seemed to be enjoying himself. And he was confident; Aubrey didn't like that. "Ain't done nothing," he repeated obstinately, as he had been doing since he was a snub-nosed ten-year-old forty years ago.

Rushton smiled. He looked to Aubrey like the police Alsatian which had once apprehended him at the back of

Woolworths in Monmouth. He said, "Where was your van on the night of the tenth of November, Aubrey?"

Aubrey swallowed, tried to allow himself time to think, then tried to stop his pulses as they began to race. November the tenth was last Saturday. The night when that stuck-up bugger from next door, Ted Giles, had been murdered. The night those two plainclothes blokes had spoken to him about, last Tuesday morning. Bloody hell! Bloody, bloody hell! "My van was parked behind the flats, I expect, as usual." He knew very well where it had been, but it was instinctive in him to be vague or dishonest when speaking to the police.

"And where were you?"

Aubrey peered at Rushton suspiciously, then glanced at the equally unrevealing face of the woman behind him. "What time you talking about?"

"Let's say between eight and twelve."

"I was in the pub, wasn't I? I always am on a Saturday night. Always have a bit of a bevvy, we do, on Saturdays."

"Usually, Aubrey, not always. Sometimes you have work to do on a Saturday night. Breaking into warehouses, that sort of thing." Rushton had done his homework on Bass's criminal record before he had him brought up from the cells.

Bass glared at him sullenly. "Well, I was in the pub last Saturday night. The Red Lion, most of the time, but I think we finished up in the White Hart. Good night we had, too. A lot of beer and a few laughs."

"Really. There'll be people who can confirm this for us, will there? People who will be willing to swear in court that you were with them for all of those four hours?

117

People willing to put their own heads on the block to tell us that you didn't slip away for half an hour or so?"

Aubrey licked his lips at the mention of a court of law. He didn't like the way this was moving. The police were always truculent with people like him. But this bastard Rushton spoke like a man with four aces in his hand. And suddenly his own friends seemed not friends at all, but blokes he met up with to drink and thieve. They wouldn't take kindly to being involved with the police on his behalf, however much he needed them. He scratched himself vigorously under both arms. "Wasn't with the same set of mates all night, was I? People came and went." He realised with a sinking heart that it was actually true. The floor seemed to be dropping away beneath his feet. He looked for succour to the woman behind the aggressive Rushton. She was smiling at him in exactly the same way as her Inspector. Even in Aubrey's broadly cast imaginings, Sergeant Ruth David no longer looked a good lay.

She said calmly, as though it was a piece of good advice which had just occurred to her, "Well, it seems you'd better find someone, Mr Bass. Someone who can speak reliably about your movements on that Saturday night."

Aubrey tried desperately to get some conviction into his voice. "I told you. I was in the pub all that night. Well, till closing time. Then we went on to a bloke's house."

Rushton's grin became a derisive leer. "Pubs, you said just now."

"Pubs, then. But that's where I was, whether there's

118

anyone to say so or not. You can't fit me up with any burglary. You'll have to find some other poor bastard."

"Oh, it's not a burglary, Aubrey. Nothing as petty as that for the new Mr Bass. We're talking murder here."

Aubrey shut his eyes for a moment, trying to stop the room spinning. The walls still did not seem stable when he opened them. His voice emerged as a whine. "Murder? You mean Ted Giles, don't you? I ain't done no murder, Mr Rushton."

"You're claiming you're just an accessory? Penalties are still severe, Aubrey. Might as well admit the whole thing and get it over with, I'd say."

Aubrey Bass saw nothing except the gravely satisfied faces opposite him; male and female, they nodded gravely in unison, as if worked by the same hand. He shouted desperately, "I'm saying I had nothing to do with any murder! That I know nothing about it! That I never saw Ted bloody Giles last Saturday night!"

Rushton seemed to find these denials amusing. Then he spoke in a tone which was suddenly hard as granite. "We found fibres from the dead man's sweater on the floor of your van, Aubrey. Hairs, too, which I dare say forensic will prove are those of the late Edward Giles. I'd say his body was taken to the churchyard at Broughton's Ash last Saturday night in the back of your van. And I'd say it was time you were thinking about that brief, Mr Bass."

Ten

T he forensics of crime are an ever-widening field. DNA testing may be the best-publicised leap forward in crime detection, but it is only part of the complex possibilities of modern technology. Almost all of the people who assist the police are civilians, and the need for specialists means that an increasing use is made of part-time expertise, bought in as and when it is necessary.

David Browne was an example of this. He was a mildmannered man of thirty-five, slightly old fashioned in both his dress and his opinions. A briar pipe was never far from his mouth, though more often than not it was unlit. His full-time work was with the BBC in Bristol; he was responsible for the monitoring of sound quality and volume levels in radio broadcasts, an unseen, rarely considered, but vital factor in the listening public's enjoyment of their programmes. For most of his days, he sat, with or without his headphones, in his sound-proof booth in Bristol, listening to recordings before they were put on the air, making occasional small adjustments to ensure the audience he never saw would receive them at their best.

And occasionally, in the evenings or at a weekend, he

helped the police. David had never turned down a request for assistance from their forensic department. Most of what he did for the BBC was necessary but repetitive; what came to him through the police was both varied and interesting. He was a man always happier to be dealing with data than people, and the forensic tasks did not disturb that pattern, but he often saw a direct outcome to them, in the arrests and trials of criminals. He followed the court reportage of his cases secretly but avidly.

This Saturday, David Browne had been presented with a task which both intrigued and excited him. The Rendezvous agency had taken to asking its new clients to record short statements about their backgrounds and requirements. The ostensible reason was to offer potential partners a sample of the voice and aspirations of the speaker. In fact, the recordings were rarely used for this purpose: the real object was to record the requirements of clients, so that they could be played back to them at a later date if the clients objected to the partners or escorts they had been offered. The procedure also ensured, of course, that the agency had a collection of tapes which could be highly embarrassing for those who had registered with Rendezvous without telling their existing spouses or partners. It was surprising how often the mere mention of the recordings served to suppress complaints about the agency's service or charges.

David Browne knew none of this. Nor did he receive any account of the threats and cajolery with which Bert Hook had extracted the tapes from Pat Roberts, manager of Rendezvous, a.k.a. Patricia Rawlings, sometime occupant of one of Her Majesty's prisons. That was not his concern: his business was to listen to the tapes with his headphones on and apply his knowledge and experience to them. Repeatedly, and through a range of amplifiers and volumes. Comparing each one with the police recording of the voice of the hysterical woman who had first told the police to contact the escort agency.

David Browne was good at his work. And he found it was of absorbing interest, repaying the intense concentration he had to give to it. Over and over again, he played and replayed the few urgent phrases on the police recording of the call from the public box:

". . . Ted Bloody Giles. Paper says he's a bloody saint. You find out about his work with Rendezvous, then see if you think he's such a fucking saint!"

He played individual words, even individual syllables, over and over again, comparing vowels, consonants and inflections with those on the eight individual tapes which the police had brought to him from the agency. He eliminated five of these quite easily, then a sixth after a couple more hearings. It took him half an hour of intense concentration before he decided between the last two of the innocent-looking cassettes from Rendezvous.

These were rough recordings, made with a poor microphone, by those with little or no experience. But that was a help rather than a hindrance to him in this work. The breathy hesitations and nervous delivery made it all the easier to isolate the peculiar variations which made each voice almost as individual as a fingerprint to this expert listener. At the end of his work, David Browne was confident enough of his findings to swear to them in court, if that should be needed at some future date. He went to the phone with real excitement: he hadn't been told exactly what his findings might mean to the woman he had now identified, but he did know that he was involved in his first murder inquiry.

It was a Saturday night, but he didn't hesitate to ring. This might be vital evidence he held in his hand: he checked the name scrawled on the cassette again as the phone shrilled at the other end of the line. Superintendent Lambert answered himself, as he had hoped. David Browne said. "I have a name for your anonymous caller, Mr Lambert." He hesitated, then plunged in first with his supplementary information, unable to resist the opportunity to parade his expertise. "She speaks something very near Standard English – but no one does that exactly. I think you'll find she comes from the north of England – almost certainly north Lancashire or south Cumbria. It's surprising how the vowels flatten out under the pressure of emotion. And I'd say from the stresses and the inflections that she's a woman who doesn't habitually use obscenities."

Lambert listened with a professional patience. Then he said quietly, "That could be helpful. And you have a name for us, Mr Browne?"

"Yes. Assuming the agency has labelled the cassette correctly, it's a woman named Zoe Ross."

John Lambert was up quite early on Sunday morning, but he found that his wife had already been out to the greenhouse and cut some of his chrysanthemums. They were one of the interests he was preparing for his eventual retirement. "Eventual" was his word; Christine had recently switched from "inevitable" to "forthcoming".

"You should be resting, not up at this time on a Sunday," he grumbled as he began his cereal.

Christine turned from arranging the flowers in a vase at the sink. "And are you going to sit around for the rest of the day, in view of your advancing age and seniority?" she said. "I'm not dying, John. I'm waiting for an operation, that's all."

He looked up at her round face, which was animated by its brief exposure to the cool air of early winter. It looked rosy with health beside the smooth yellow spheres of the inflexed chrysanthemum flowers. In the paradoxical way of these things, she seemed healthier and stronger since they had received the news that she needed serious surgery. He was aware that he was merely playing out the ritual of protest as he said, "You do need to rest, you know. To make sure your body is in the strongest possible condition for the shock of the operation."

"Ah! The way to do that is to take moderate exercise. Being up before my husband and cutting a few flowers hardly rates as that."

He switched tactics. "Did you have the pain again last night?"

She could not lie to him, even after all these years. "A little, yes. But it doesn't worry me. Not since I found out what it was. Dr Cooper said I should expect it, when I was tired at the end of the day. It's nothing to get very alarmed about, a bit of angina."

125

"Well, it alarms me. You're too active for your own good."

"All right, lord and master, I shall obey." She turned towards him as he sat awkwardly at the small kitchen table with his cereal spoon in his hand and dropped into an ironic curtsey. It was one of the gestures of their youth, one of the gestures she had used then to end more serious arguments than this. She had been a lithe and graceful kitten when he first knew her. Now she was stiffer, almost losing her balance as she bent low and spread her skirt with both hands. She laughed it away, but he was suddenly seared by the passing years and the inevitable end of their human foolery.

"I shall rest presently, with that fat Sunday paper, and in due course you will bring me morning coffee. If you're going to be here, of course; resting your ageing bones; following your own counsel." She knew he wasn't, he realised. He gave her a weary grin, which acknowledged that he had lost the argument; he hoped it told her also that he loved her. It was a lot to expect of that briefest of smiles, he reflected, as he drove through the lanes to collect Bert Hook. If he ever wrote his memoirs in retirement, as he was often urged to do, Christine would figure less prominently than she should.

John Lambert knew his literature well enough to be aware how difficult it is to make virtue interesting.

It was exactly a week since old Tom Dodds had found the body of Edward Giles in the churchyard at Broughton's Ash. As Lambert left the village where Hook lived and drove his old Vauxhall over an ancient stone bridge, the

Wye gleamed briefly beneath them, its swirling winter waters illuminated as they caught and reflected the pale lemon of the winter sun.

He had made no apology for disturbing the woman's Sunday. If she had complained, he would have told her more tersely than he had his wife that murder waits for no man. As they drove into the suburbs of Oldford, he was intensely aware of the statistic which asserts that half of the murder cases in which there has been no arrest within the first week remain on the files unsolved.

Zoe Ross did not complain. Bert Hook had phoned to arrange this meeting, and she must have been watching for the car, for the door of the house was open before they could ring the bell. She was no more than thirty, and possibly even younger; with her slender figure, her pony-tailed hair and her small, delicate features, it was difficult to tell. Lambert watched her as he produced his warrant card and introduced Hook and himself. He was certain she was nervous, but that didn't necessarily mean much.

She said, "Sergeant Hook wouldn't tell me why you wanted to speak to me. But it's about Ted, isn't it? You'd better come in." She turned abruptly and led them into a tidy sitting room where walls were covered with water colours and the *Observer* lay neatly folded upon a coffee table. She gestured towards a large sofa, then sat and curled her legs beneath her on the room's single armchair by the fireplace. She moved well, but she was like a dancer following choreographed steps, playing out a dance which was meant to convey that she had nothing to fear.

Lambert said, "I'll come straight to the point. We need to know the details of your relationship with Mr Giles."

"Need to know? That's a strong phrase, Superintendent. What right have you to demand that I reveal everything about a private relationship to strangers?"

"The rights conferred by a murder inquiry." Lambert was suddenly impatient with this supple and alert young woman. Perhaps, thinking of the wife he had left so recently, he was intolerant of her very youth and energy. "We don't like anonymous phone calls, Miss Ross. They cause us a lot of trouble."

"I suppose they must, but I fail to see—"

"I'll save you the embarrassment of further lying. We know that it was you who made the anonymous phone call to Oldford CID at 6.13 p.m. on Thursday last. It would have saved a lot of time and expense if you had given your name at that time."

If he had been looking to shake her, he had succeeded. Her slim torso recoiled against the back of her chair as if she was dodging a physical blow. "You can't know that I made that call."

"Miss Ross, I can assure you that we do. It was recorded, and there are means of establishing that it was your voice. What we are interested in now is why you made it."

The bright, unlined face had turned pale. She reached out her hand to the table beside her, seeking for something to occupy her hands. Anything would have done, but she fixed unseeingly on the remote control for her hi-fi system. For the next few minutes of their conversation, it turned over and over between the slender fingers, unremarked but perhaps in some small way therapeutic. She said softly, "I'm sorry. I was overcome with grief when I made that phone call. Anonymous letters or messages are not my normal way. It was a desperate measure: I've never made a call like that before."

"But it wasn't just grief that made you ring, was it? There were other emotions involved. If I played the tape to you now, you'd understand what I mean."

She shuddered, as if she feared that he might actually produce the evidence and make her listen to it. "Yes, you're right. I was jealous. For three days I couldn't get my head round Ted's death at all. And when I heard it was murder, I suppose I wanted it to be her."

"By 'her' you mean Mrs Constance Elson?"

She nodded. For a moment her voice took on the bitterness of the phone call, though not its high-pitched hysteria. "Connie Bloody Elson, that's right! With her money and her clothes and her bungalow and her ever-available, all-consuming body. Connie the nyphomaniac python!" They caught now the slight flattening of the vowels, the trace of northern accent, that David Browne had pinpointed for them in his analysis of her taped voice. She began to weep, silently but copiously, and they knew in that moment that these were phrases she had hurled unavailingly at the living Ted Giles in this very room.

Lambert watched her silently, as objectively as a scientist with a specimen under a microscope, devoid in his professional capacity of the social promptings of embarrassment. In the silence, he was busy with his own concerns: the woman wasn't acting this; therefore at the time of Giles's death, she had plainly been jealous to the point of distraction; therefore she might well have been even more bitter about Ted Giles's behaviour than that of Connie Elson; therefore she might well have been unbalanced enough to have killed the man she saw as wronging her. The measured words of Saunders, the pathologist, came back to him from the beginning of the case: "He was garrotted, probably taken from behind with a thin wire . . . With the implement used, this could easily have been done by a woman, if the victim was taken by surprise."

Lambert waited for the face wet with tears to lift towards him before he said, "So you were jealous of Mrs Elson. But you didn't direct our attention specifically to her, did you? You told us to investigate Rendezvous."

"Yes. I wasn't seeing things very clearly, but I thought that any of the women who had seen Ted through the agency might have been involved in his death." She smiled a bitter, self-deprecating smile. "He was a very attractive man, Ted, and I suppose I thought that anyone who felt as possessive about him as I did might have killed him."

He smiled back, wondering how clearly she understood that she had just stated her own case to be a suspect. "You were a Rendezvous client yourself, Miss Ross. We heard the tape on which you described yourself and what you wanted from the agency."

Her eyes widened as she looked him full in the face for the first time since they had begun to speak. "That's how you found out that I had made the phone call to CID on Thursday, wasn't it? I'd forgotten that I'd even recorded that cassette for that hard-faced bitch."

"Is that how you met Ted Giles? Through a meeting arranged by the agency?"

For a moment she was puzzled. Then her face cleared and she looked for a moment as if she would laugh. "No. Of course you would think that, when you found me on their books, but it wasn't like that at all. I met Ted over a year ago at a union meeting – I teach Art in Gloucester. We were attracted to each other immediately and we quickly began a long-term relationship. Oh, I can see from your faces that you have your doubts about that, and I can guess how things look to you now, but that's how it was. I knew pretty quickly that Ted had been involved in working for Rendezvous as an escort. I was shocked at first, but pleased that he'd told me – it meant we were being honest with each other, I thought."

She stopped abruptly, clearly thinking about this moment of intimacy from many months ago. Lambert had to prompt her with, "But he didn't give up the work with Rendezvous, did he?"

"No. He said he was going to. Then I found two months later that it was still going on."

"Yet you didn't finish with him there and then. If what you are telling us is true, you are asking us to believe that you are a very forbearing woman, Miss Ross."

Sitting still with her legs curled beneath her in the big armchair, her hair a little ruffled over a face still wet with tears but devoid of make-up, she looked pretty, vulnerable, younger than her years despite her distress. She said, as though the phrase explained everything, "I was a woman in love, Superintendent Lambert. And I was more clear-sighted than you might think. Ted was a man to whom money was important, and I knew that. He'd grown up in grinding poverty, with a father who was often ill and out of work. Rendezvous to him meant lots of money without much effort, and he didn't find it as easy as I had thought it would be to turn away from that. We had a blazing row when I found he was still taking money from them."

But that row still hadn't stopped his activities, whatever she thought. Lambert, using the neutral language of bureaucracy to turn the knife, said, "We have reason to believe that Edward Giles was still receiving payments from Rendezvous at the time of his death."

He had thought that she would deny it, might even fly into a rage at him. Instead, she nodded bleakly and said, "I know. I joined Rendezvous myself purely to find out exactly what was going on. The girl at the desk showed me some photographs of escorts and I picked out Ted's. She let me glance at his file to see his background. That's how I found out about Mrs Connie Bloody Elson and her designs on my man."

"He was going to marry her?"

"No!" The monosyllable rang like a shot in that quiet, tasteful room. "She thought he was. But that's as far as it went. He was going to marry me. I'm not defending the way he behaved, the way he deceived other women, but that's the way he was. I'd have changed him, given time, but I won't have the chance now."

The old female belief, noble but mistaken, that they could change the men they loved, that the rogue could be taken out and the hero enlarged. Lambert had heard it too often to be surprised by it when an intelligent woman voiced it. He kept his face impassive, devoid of any hint of cynicism, as Zoe Ross lapsed again into tears. Then he said, "Forgive me, but I must ask you this. If you were so sure that he was going to marry you, why should you be so resentful of Mrs Elson? From what you say, she was being exploited by Ted Giles, but she didn't represent a threat to you."

She sighed, acknowledging with her slender, ballerina's hands that it was a fair point. "I suppose she represented the whole tawdry world of Rendezvous. And if I'm honest, those things in Ted which I saw and didn't like. She offered all the wealth he craved – and she was good in bed. He made no bones about that. But he was going to marry me. When I heard he'd been murdered, my first thought was that it was a jealous woman who had done it. Someone who had hoped to have him permanently, and then found out that he was going to marry me and give up the easy pickings. Connie, or just possibly one of the other women who had enjoyed his favours through Rendezvous."

But that argument could just as easily be turned on its head, thought the two men who sat on Zoe Ross's fashionable sofa. If she had found out that he proposed to continue playing the rewarding field at the agency, or that he was opting for marriage to the wealth and opulent charms of Connie Elson, the slender woman opposite might have taken her own passionate revenge. Lambert glanced at Hook, and that stolid figure looked up from his notes and asked calmly, "Where were you on the night of Saturday the tenth of November, Miss Ross?"

Her face showed that she knew the reason for the question. "Here. I was waiting for Ted, but he never came."

Or he came and met his Nemesis in the form of a steel wire tightening round his throat, thought Lambert. He said, "Do you know a man named Aubrey Bass? A neighbour of Ted's."

"His next-door neighbour? Creepy sort of bloke with a beer gut? He used to watch me coming and going, when I first knew Ted."

"That's the man."

"Well, I know him, then. Just about. He leered at me once or twice when I was on my way into Ted's flat. Made it pretty clear his athlete's body was available to me if I should require it. He kept some pretty unsavoury company, according to Ted. Haven't seen him for months. Why?"

"I can't tell you that."

But Zoe Ross knew Bass, by her own admission. Had known him for months. Had all but indicated that he might not be above acting as an accessory in the disposal of a corpse, if the price was right. "Please don't leave the area without letting us have an address," said Lambert as they left.

She nodded dutifully in the doorway of her house, understanding the implications of what they said, see-mingly not frightened by the injunction. They would have given a lot to see her face in the moments after she had shut the door of the house upon them.

Eleven

It was Lambert who took the decision to release Aubrey Bass.

In truth, there was little the police could do to hold him for much longer. They had already kept him in custody overnight and for the whole of Sunday morning on suspicion of his involvement in a serious crime. It would have been necessary to charge him to keep him longer, and they had not been able to add to the initial forensic findings that his van had been used for the transfer of the corpse of Edward Giles to the churchyard at Broughton's Ash on the night of November 10th. A known associate of Bass's, a petty thief called Alf Chetwood, had said when questioned that Aubrey had been drinking with him for three hours on that Saturday evening, a period which amply covered the times when a white van had been sighted by the residents of Brompton's Ash.

No policeman would give any credence to the word of Alf Chetwood, but his evidence would have the same standing in a court of law as that of the most upright citizen. More to the point, successive attempts had failed to shake the story of Aubrey Bass himself. He had been questioned at intervals by Rushton, Hook and Lambert. He had dithered; he had scratched himself with increasing vigour; he had filled his cell and a series of interview rooms with nervous flatulence.

But he had not changed his story. His van had been parked behind the flats where he lived, in its usual place. For the whole of the night of November 10th, as far as he knew. If anyone had used it that night, it certainly wasn't him. For a man who normally switched his ground under police pressure and whined his way into trouble like the petty crook he was, Bass held to his story with remarkable consistency. As he shifted himself from buttock to buttock and scratched beneath each arm in turn, it began to seem that Aubrey Bass might for once be telling the truth.

Rushton told him he was being released because he was a health hazard to the whole station, and sent him on his way. Aubrey essayed a little truculence and tried to speak loftily of the dire consequences for the police of wrongful arrest, but it emerged too shakily to give even him any satisfaction. He made noises about the return of his van, trudged homeward with a weary relief, and shut the door of his flat upon the world.

Although it was still early in the afternoon and no one could see into the windows of his first-floor flat, he drew the curtains before he made his call to Alf Chetwood. "Thanks, Alf. Do the same for you, you know. Have done, haven't I?" Might as well let him know it was a favour called in rather than a debt to be repaid. "We mustn't let the bastards grind us down."

They went through a ritual denunciation of the police, crowed a little at their small frustration of the activities of the filth. Then Alf asked what they had being trying to frame him for, and Aubrey became evasive. Murder was right outside their league, and the mention of it brought a chill even to their dubious world. And there was no need to tell Alf how big a favour his lie had been.

After he had fufilled his obligations of gratitude, Aubrey opened a can of beer to wash away the taste of the police cell, belched loudly and extravagantly in the privacy of his kitchen, as if to convince himself that he was free, and sat down in front of his television set to make ready for the afternoon's football on Sky.

When the knock came at his door, he wondered for a moment whether to ignore it. But if it was the fuzz again, he knew they certainly wouldn't go away. With a weary curse, he laboured himself out of the battered armchair and went to the door.

It wasn't the police. It was quite the prettiest face he had seen for some time, with a lithe young body beneath it, and Aubrey was glad to have both of them within his walls. Zoe Ross perched on a dining chair opposite Aubrey Bass, keeping her delectable knees fastidiously together. "We need to talk," she said.

Colin Pitman hunched his big shoulders against the rising wind as he went reluctantly out to the garage. Though it was scarcely six o'clock, it was already very dark. There was no sign of a moon, and the low, racing clouds obscured any light the stars might have given him. He hunched himself over the steering wheel of the Jaguar

XK8, allowed himself an ill-humoured oath, and turned the key to roar the great engine into life.

Even now, when he was threatened, the sound of that engine, with its six cylinders roaring like a caged beast before they settled to a smooth, powerful purr, brought him a little thrill of pleasure, natural to a man who had dealt with engines and machinery for all of his successful working life. The Jaguar was one of the few tangible badges of success he allowed himself to wear for others, and its engine note was the quiet, half-conscious assurance to himself that he was a success in his work. Even tonight, the quiet power of the XK8 gave him a tiny injection of confidence, as he eased the big car onto the A449 and drove northwards. Yet that was soon submerged under his anxiety and rage. Colin Pitman was a man not used to being summoned to meetings against his will.

Indeed, it was a long time since anyone had made this man do anything: he controlled his own destiny and was proud of it. Yet tonight he didn't see how he could have done anything else – even now he didn't, though he had thought of nothing else in the hour since the phone call had come. Over the last thirty years, he had made bluntness a virtue, had scorned those who refused to face facts, who made issues more complicated than they were. Basically Pitman was honest and straightforward, in both his business and his personal dealings. His late wife had often complained with irritated affection that he was *too* straightforward, too determined upon logic, that he refused to see the complexities of any problem. He would have liked to be able to talk to her now, for he felt confused as well as angry. He was realising that a single rash act brought in its wake a whole series of dilemmas he had not expected.

As he drove into the outskirts of Worcester, he became aware why the man had chosen this time and this place. The warehouse lay alongside other such buildings, at the end of a cul de sac, and at this time on a Sunday night there seemed to be not a light in the entire area. There was a stretch of old cobbles from an earlier era to the right of the high doors of the place. Pitman resolved that if the man had others with him he would swing the Jaguar in a tight circle and race away. You could not build up a business in haulage without making enemies, and whatever reasons lay behind this strange summons he was not going to risk an ambush in this deserted place.

But the fierce headlights of the Jaguar picked out a single figure, pressing back automatically against the door of the warehouse, shielding its eyes against the blinding glare of the twin beams. Pitman stopped the car, keeping the engine running, letting its power die to an idling that was almost inaudible within its leather interior. He considered for a moment whether he should beckon the man over, conduct this exchange on his own terms from within his own cave of warmth. Then he switched the engine off and climbed out stiffly into the cold night air. He didn't intend that there should be any violence, but if there was, he wanted to be standing balanced upon his own two feet. Pitman gripped the length of heavy piping in the pocket of his car coat as he went towards the suddenly scarcely visible figure in the shadow of the warehouse entry.

"You'd better have good reason to get me here like this, Matt Walsh," he rasped.

He had left the lights on in the Jaguar, but the head-lights had switched off automatically when he removed the keys from the ignition. As his eyes became accustomed to the dimmer light of the sidelights, the man turned half towards him and he saw the face he recognised. A thin face with a prominent nose; birdlike, crafty, sidelong, as though it was meant to be seen perpetually in profile. "Tis I, indeed, Mr Pitman. And I alone, as I said it would be, d'you see." The voice had a familiar, wheedling tone, and Pitman was suddenly nauseated that it should have brought him here like this.

He had sacked this Irishman a year ago, for tampering with his tachometer, and lying on his returns about the mileage and the hours that he had been driving. Suddenly he hated both this man and himself for being here with him. He did not trouble to keep the loathing out of his voice as he said, "You were sacked fair and square, Walsh! You and I have nothing more to say to each other." Yet even as he said it, he knew it couldn't be true. Else why would he be here, at the behest of this pathetic creature?

"You've put your finger on it, sure an' all, Mr Pitman. I want my old job back, drivin' the lorries for you. Nothing more than that." The wheedling tone of the voice overrode the Irish accent, even now, when Matt Walsh was trying to dictate terms. Pitman was the strong man here and Walsh was the subordinate, and not just in physical terms. The big man was used to controlling his world and those who inhabited it; the slight figure beside him was a natural follower.

Yet it was Walsh who was in control, who had set up the time and the place for this meeting, and Pitman knew that even as he said roughly, "And why should I give you that? I told you, you were sacked fair and square!" He repeated the phrase harshly, as if the justice of the man's dismissal could carry weight, even now when he had put himself in the creature's power.

"I know where you were on Saturday night, the tenth of November, d'you see?" Walsh iterated his one precious fact carefully, almost apologetically.

Almost as if it were not a threat, thought Colin Pitman bitterly. His hands were thrust into his pockets, and the fingers of the right one closed now upon the length of piping. He wanted to hit this sly, wiry man alongside him, to express his outrage that he should be threatened by this contemptible presence. But that would solve nothing – would lead indeed to greater problems.

Unless he killed him.

For a moment he toyed with the thought. Then he was appalled by it. Had it come to this then? Had he been reduced to this? For a searing moment he longed for the wife who was dead, who would have guided his conduct in the first place, who would have made sure that he would never put himself in a position to be threatened by the likes of Matt Walsh. Then he said dully, "And if I give you a job, what then? Will you be in to my office every time the going gets rough, threatening me again, wanting your own way, wanting more money?"

"Indeed that I won't, Mr Pitman. You'll have my word on that. A job driving the lorries again, and you'll hear no more from me, you won't." With the recognition that he had probably won, there was an earnestness now in Walsh's whining, a relief that he should be back in his natural position of supplication. "I swear you won't, Mr Pitman. It's just that I need the job, you see."

A blackmailer apologising, thought Pitman sourly. For he was being blackmailed, and both of them knew it. He said heavily. "You're lying, Walsh, just as you lied last year, about your mileages. You can't know where I was on that Saturday night, because I was at home." Even as he said it, he knew it could not be true: a man like Walsh would never have dared to threaten him without being sure of his ground.

The voice beneath him sounded almost regretful as it said, "It's true, Mr Pitman, really. I know where you were. Seamus Connelly saw you."

For a moment, he could not place the name. Then he realised that Connelly was an employee of his, an Irishman who drove lorries to the Continent, right across into Eastern Europe on occasions. He said dully, as if it was a proof that he could not have been seen, "But Connelly was on holiday at the time. He only took out his first load again on Friday."

"Yes, but he saw you. There's no doubt of it, Mr Pitman." The nervous voice came out of the darkness as if the words gave the speaker pain. There was a stink of bad breath, a whiff of the whisky which had steeled the speaker to this task.

Colin Pitman paused, forcing himself to think with something nearer to his normal clearness. He could ask for assurances, guarantees that this wouldn't go any further, that once this repellent creature was back in his employment there would be no further mention of this, no further exploitation of the knowledge Walsh held about that fateful night. Such assurances would not be worth the bad breath that voiced them. He thrust his clenched fists against the lining at the bottom of his pockets, fearing that if they came out they would grasp the throat of the puny, insistent man who trembled in the darkness beside him. Then he said, forcing the words out as his voice grated with his reluctance, "All right. You can have your job back. Come into the office tomorrow afternoon. I'll make sure they're expecting you by then. But if you ever breathe a word of this to a living soul, you're a dead man, damn you!"

"Oh, it won't go any further, Mr Pitman, so help me God it won't! It's none of my business, and it will be forgotten. Sure it's just that I need the job, you see, or I'd never have raised it at all, honest I wouldn't!"

With his aim achieved, Walsh was only too anxious to get away. Colin Pitman had only seen blackmailers on film, and they had always been truculent and confident. You could not have had a more unaggressive enforcement than this, he thought sourly. He dismissed the man, as if he and not Walsh had been in control, and the small figure scuttled away. Like a rat bolting into the darkness, thought Colin bitterly. He heard a small car engine fire twice before it struggled into reluctant life a hundred yards or so away.

Pitman stayed where he was for two minutes, until the notes of that engine died away in the distance. He knew as he went slowly back to his Jaguar that it was the man in the expensive clothes and the big car who had made the concessions here. The six cylinders of the four-litre engine purred into life at the first touch of the switch.

For the first time, the noise did not give him the accustomed small thrill of comfortable contentment.

Twelve

I n almost thirty years as a policeman, John Lambert had trained himself to remain calm whatever the situation. But the unexpected could still shock him.

And he was not prepared for the hospital crest on the stark white foolscap envelope as he gathered up the post on Monday morning. He felt his heart pounding as he resisted the urge to open the letter himself, to protect the wife who seemed now so vulnerable, after being for so many years the rock to which his family was tethered. Christine was sitting at the table as he took the post into the warm kitchen. "I think your letter from the hospital's come," he said. He wondered at the banality of the words; his voice sounded strangely high and brittle in his own ears.

She smiled up at him, slit the envelope with the slim, expert fingers which he had watched at a thousand household tasks over the years, handed him the sheet he now could not bring himself to read. "I'm to go in tomorrow," she said. "That probably means they'll operate on Wednesday, all being well."

A curious phrase that, in these circumstances, he thought. He said, "It's too soon. You need to build up your strength. You're not ready for it."

She laughed. "You mean you're not, don't you, John? I'm as ready as I'll ever be."

"But the tests – they can't be certain yet that you—"

"They did the tests the week before last, John. I'm all right – ready for the surgery. The sooner the better, I say. Get it done now, I'll be ready to enjoy the spring. Might even drag you away for a holiday."

The spring seemed impossibly far away to her husband. He said, "It's a big step, heart surgery. Still a big step, even with all the advances. You haven't had time to think about it properly."

"I've thought about little else for the past few days, you great booby! I'm ready. Or I will be, when I've packed my bag and made arrangements to make sure my helpless husband survives while I'm having a good rest in hospital. Speaking of which, be off with you to work and let me get on with it!"

She had almost to push him through the front door of the bungalow. He was just a big, vulnerable child, she thought, as she waved to his anxious, affectionate face as he reversed the old Vauxhall out of the garage and drove away.

It was a relief to drop the wide, unworried smile. It could stay in the kitchen drawer with the cutlery until John came home in the evening and she needed it again. She picked up the phone and dialled her daughter's number. "Jacky? The letter's come. I've to go in tomorrow. That means they'll be operating on Wednesday, I think."

"So soon? How do you feel, Mum?"

"Apprehensive, to be honest."

"Of course you do. Shall I come over?"

"No, I'll drive over to you. I'd like to see the children. But I'll come while they're still at school. Then I can be frightened for an hour, in peace. And you can give me tea and sympathy. Or better still, gin and sympathy. I need a bit of Dutch courage to be cheerful again for your dad tonight."

She put the phone down and went and looked at the wedding photograph in the dining room, with a young John Lambert standing erect and protective beside that strange, pretty young woman who shyly held his arm.

All men were just children really, in the most important things.

Two days after the Coroner's Court jury had brought in a verdict of murder by person or persons unknown, the coroner released the body of Edward Giles for a funeral.

It was unusual, but the Oldfield coroner was a kindly man of much experience, aware of the community around him in a way an urban official might not have been. He was mindful of the feelings of relatives, of the need people felt to mark the end of formal grief with the ritual of a funeral. The deceased had died by asphyxiation caused by a piece of wire drawn tight around his throat; that was clear and hardly open to dispute, even by the most ingenious of defence counsels. There scarcely seemed the need to preserve the right for a second postmortem by a pathologist retained by the lawyers for the defence. Discreet enquiries by the coroner's officer revealed that a burial, not a cremation, was planned for

147

Giles. An exhumation would still be possible, in the highly unlikely event of its being required.

So it was that on the morning of Monday, November 19th, Bert Hook found himself trying to make his considerable bulk unnoticeable in the Catholic Church of St Alban's, Oldford. "Just pop in and keep your eyes open!" Lambert had said, as if there was nothing to it. In truth, it was easier for Hook to escape notice than most of his colleagues. With his rubicund countenance and comfortable girth, he put most people more in mind of a publican or a farmer than a policeman. He set himself between two of the regular parishioners, towards the rear of the church. There he shrank into his dark grey overcoat and clutched his hymnal reverently. Even those people whom he had interviewed in connection with this death – and there were five of them there – did not remark him as they passed by him and moved to the more prominent pews at the front of the modern, brick-built church.

Hook, who was as usual far more observant than those around him realised, noted varying degrees of grief in the principal participants in this ritual. The estranged wife of the deceased, sitting beside her father in the foremost of the family benches, gave little sign of emotion. Sue Giles watched impassively as the coffin of her husband was brought to the front for its final blessing from the priest. Standing beside her, the bearlike figure of her father, Colin Pitman, gripped his daughter's slim arm in its covering of expensive black coat as the coffin arrived, as if to offer support. She smiled up at him reassuringly, and her father forced a small, answering smile onto his

148

broad, nervous face. It was a moment of intimacy between the two, but Hook felt the gestures marked a further stage along her road to independence rather than any real grief and consolation.

The impression was reinforced by the contrast between the demeanour of the wife and that of Ted Giles's mother in the bench behind her. The poor woman was weeping silently and struggling to maintain some kind of control, whilst her husband offered her what support he could from the trials of his own grief. The worst funerals of all were always the ones where the parents were still around to see their child interred. Bert Hook had seen it before, but his heart was always wrenched by the sight. He forced his attention away to study the reactions of others in this near-silent drama.

If the movements of Sue Giles were under strict control, the actions and reactions of the other two women who interested Hook were more revealing. Connie Elson, the woman who claimed Ted Giles had been intending to marry her, arrived ten minutes before the coffin, stalked to the front of the church, looked with a flash of contempt at the benches set aside for family mourners on the right, and established herself in the first pew on the left of the aisle. She was erect and proud as she marched past the unnoticed Hook, clad in a straight black coat whose only decoration was jet beading down the front. She had a broad black hat which some might have considered rather too dashing for a funeral, black high-heeled shoes, and black silk gloves. When she passed Hook, he noted that she was made up carefully, discreetly, and no doubt expensively.

When the coffin arrived and she turned herself briefly towards it whilst the priest recited the opening prayers, he saw that she was weeping. The mask given to her by her make-up was washed away, and in profile she looked all of her forty-six years, the oldest and perhaps the most tragic of the three women who had been in their different ways close to Ted Giles, and who had as a result been drawn into the investigation of his murder. To Bert's mind, her unashamed grief gave her a particular dignity, as she held herself erect within the strange tableau at the front of the church. He felt a sudden, unprofessional shaft of pity for this woman, seemingly the most vulnerable all the people involved in this strange case. She might well be the richest of the three, but Bert fancied she was going to have the emptiest life, after this was over. Even if she wasn't locked away as the killer of her lover: Hook, who doubted if Ted Giles would ever have married her, made that automatic reservation.

In appearance at least, the third woman involved could hardly have presented a greater contrast. Where Sue Giles was low-key, watchful, correct, and Connie Elson was a weeping monolith of grief, Zoe Ross might have dressed for a shopping trip rather than a funeral. She arrived, breathless but relieved, no more than a minute before the pall-bearers brought the coffin to the front of the church. She was hatless, clad in a green coat and brown low-heeled shoes. Only the flimsy dark-blue scarf at her neck might have been seen as a concession to mourning. She moved down the aisle with swift, short steps and slid easily into the bench behind Connie Elson.

With her ponytail of shining brown hair, her supple and graceful movements, her slender, athletic figure, she might almost have been the daughter of the more statuesque figure in black in front of her. She certainly looked younger than her thirty years. Hook had to remind himself that this composed young woman was the same one who had come to their notice because she had screamed her jealousy and frustration at them in the obscenities of an anonymous phone call, with her emotions completely out of control.

He saw her in profile when she turned towards the coffin for the priest's opening prayers over it. She brought her hands up from her side and clasped them in prayer for the soul of Edward Giles, as the priest urged them all to do; it was a simple, unforced gesture, which in her had the force of a balletic mime. Zoe Ross had the fragility of youth and grace to set against the shuddering grief of Connie Elson. Yet Hook saw with a little pang of surprise that Zoe too was weeping, silently, with no visible movement of her slim body, like a Botticelli Venus surprised into grief.

The requiem mass proceeded, and Hook watched the three women and the single man who were his leading suspects. There was no sign of the other man who must be included in that list, Graham Reynolds. That was only to be expected: the man who plans to marry the estranged wife has no place at her husband's funeral. Bert was glad for the sake of the grief-racked parents that Graham Reynolds had chosen to remain at his post in Oldford Comprehensive. Whatever the rights and wrongs of a broken marriage, it would be difficult for them to see the man taking over from their son as anything other than an interloper at his funeral.

The school was represented by Michael Yates, the nervous young man who had talked to them about Ted Giles when they had begun their enquiries in the school. His movements were jerky, his manner gauche, but when the organist played for the hymns, he led the singing in a warm, firm tenor, which emerged with surprising power and confidence from his gangly frame. He smiled his recognition at Hook as the mourners trooped out of church behind the coffin, the only one of the people they had spoken to during the week of the investigation who acknowledged his presence.

Bert kept on the periphery of the scene at the cemetery, huddled in his overcoat againt the chill November breeze, prepared to offer conventional sympathy to any of the mourners who approached him. None did. Each seemed preoccupied with the silent, central presence of the polished coffin, as it was brought to the grave and lowered carefully on its ropes to its final place of rest. The wife stood beside the weeping parents, dutifully mute, grim rather than grieving. She threw a single pinch of earth into the grave when the box of soil was offered to her, then took a step backwards and looked no more into the hole where the body of her late husband had been laid. Instead, she stared straight ahead. Her father shook his head at the offer of soil and holy water to cast upon the coffin. Colin Pitman's thoughts were all for his daughter. He stood behind her, raising a hand to each of her shoulders, holding her as if prepared to defend her from some physical assault. She did not turn her head to look at him, but raised a single small black-clad hand and placed it over his massive bear paw.

On the opposite side of the grave, Connie Elson and Zoe Ross were separated by three other mourners. Hook watched each of them in turn take the little phial of holy water and a handful of earth and cast it upon the lid of the coffin below them. Each of them stood for a long second afterwards, looking down upon the plate with Edward Giles's name and age upon it, as if loth to take this final leave, and then stepped back, Connie Elson heavily, Zoe Ross with the same unthinking grace which seemed to inform all her movements. Probably neither of them could have seen clearly the bouquets and sprays of flowers which they dutifully inspected with the other mourners.

As far as Bert Hook could see, none of the four people he was interested in spoke a word in that sorrowing group. Yet he was sure each of them was aware of the others. And aware also that someone standing quietly beside that grave could have killed the man who lay within it.

On the Monday evening after the funeral, the man who had not attended it, Graham Reynolds, went to see Sue Giles. He walked through the ancient market town to the prosperous suburb on the outskirts where the woman he planned to marry lived. It took him only twenty minutes. He didn't use his car because cars were such a giveaway. And though there was no reason why he should not be seen consorting openly with Sue, a natural caution made him secretive about his movements.

He looked suddenly over his shoulder several times on his journey; the last occasion was when he was three-quarters of the way up the drive to the big house. There was no evidence that he had been followed. He wouldn't have put it past that steely-eyed Superintendent to have put a police tail on him – not that even the best-trained observer would have seen him doing anything he shouldn't. He and Sue had spoken on the phone, but this was the first time he had visited her since the body had been discovered and they had been questioned. Wednesday, that had been, in her case, and Thursday in his. It seemed much longer than four days ago.

Sue knew he was coming. She shut the front door quickly behind him and threw herself into his arms. They spent a long moment like that, not kissing each other, feeling the warmth of the familiar body against and around them, closing their eyes and feeling the security they brought to each other. Then he released her, kissed her briefly on the lips, and stood without letting go of her, looking down into the blue-green eyes he knew so well, sighing his relief that they should be together again.

"How was the funeral?" he said. "As difficult as you expected?"

She thought for a moment. "No, it wasn't really. It was an ordeal, of course, but not as bad as I expected. Ted's parents were terribly upset, of course. I managed to convince them I was sorry about the death without lapsing into any real hypocrisy about Ted. I didn't pretend to be grief-stricken."

He wanted to question her further about it, to convince himself that it had all gone smoothly, but he sensed that she had had enough of it. "Were the police there?" he said.

"That Sergeant was there – the one that came to see me with the Superintendent and took notes. He was at the back of the church. I didn't see him until I was coming out after the service, and I pretended I didn't recognise him then. I don't know if he went to the cemetery or not; I didn't see him there, but he might have been somewhere in the background, I suppose."

"Your dad was with you?"

"Yes. I think he thought I was going to be more upset than I was. I suspect he was quite disappointed that I didn't need more support from him to get through it."

"He's a good bloke, your dad. Very fond of you."

There was no need for him to have said that. He was stating the obvious and both of them knew it. But they found, now that they were together as for days they had longed to be, that they were talking like strangers. They went on like that for the next twenty minutes, saying polite nothings, talking like distant acquaintances who feared to stray into topics of conversation where they might have embarrassing disagreements. The death which they had thought would bring them together was at present dividing them. Both of them felt it; neither was prepared to voice the thought.

Well, it was early days yet. The image of the funeral, of the scenes when the coffin was brought into church and when she had stood with the others at the graveside, were bound to be etched firmly upon her mind's eye tonight. Graham wished that he could have been there, at her side. He felt shut out that it should have been so. But he

155

knew it wouldn't have been appropriate, that it would have been wrong if he had been there. People might have seen him as exulting in the death of his rival. And it certainly wouldn't have helped Ted's parents to see him there, while their son was set in his final resting place.

They had discussed all that before, in the days between the death and the funeral. It was silly that the absence they had agreed for him should now be intruding between them. They had several drinks, sitting together on the sofa, wondering what to say next, as they had never done before. The alcohol had little effect. Because neither of them cared to acknowledge their unexpected difficulties, they did not voice them, so that they could not laugh at the foolishness of it and change the atmosphere.

At ten o'clock, they slid into Sue's big bed and made love. It was as muted as the rest of the evening which had led to it. Neither of them spoke; they handled each other as carefully as youngsters in bed together for the first time. But without the passion which might have carried young people through, Sue thought afterwards. She lay for a while with her head crooked in his arm across the pillow, with both of them on their backs, as they had often done before. It was usually a time of great intimacy, when they talked about anything and everything, about the future they would have together. Or when they were peaceful, comfortably warm with each other, as intimate in silence as in the exuberance of the sex which had preceded this quietus.

Tonight the silence seemed more tense, as if it needed to be filled with the reassuring words which neither of them could muster. And when he rose and went away to his own home, as they had agreed it was wise that he should, it felt to both of them a squalid act, almost a betrayal. From the darkness of her bedroom, she watched him walk in the starlight down the long drive, moving quite swiftly. Too swiftly, like one glad to be away, she thought.

He did not once look back at the silent house.

Thirteen

T he late husband of Constance Elson had made money in a variety of ways. A lot of money. Most of the later ways had been legal; as he amassed a fortune, he found it easier to go on accumulating money by methods which were perfectly acceptable. He had a shrewd eye for small companies with good ideas. He moved in during the early stages, when they were in need of finance, and he drove bargains which made him a very rich man when three of these businesses eventually reached the stock market.

Archie Elson always said that it was easy to make money quite properly, once you had a certain amount of it. He went on saying so until the day he collapsed and died with his second heart attack. But he was never specific about how he had acquired his first half-million. In his more expansive and generous moments, when he had eaten well and enjoyed a few brandies, he would say rather sentimentally that you needed a good woman at your side, to provide the support and stability a successful man required. Then he would clasp the Junoesque figure of his wife tightly to his side and say that without Connie he could never have done it, and she would flush

159

becomingly and tell everyone that Archie had drunk a little too much again.

Connie was ten years younger than Archie, which helped to reinforce the impression that she was an innocent young girl who knew little of his early dealings and the dubious paths he had taken towards success. But Connie had been born in a Bristol slum with nothing. She was both more astute and more interested in the way wealth was acquired than these observers gave her credit for. When Archie was alone with her and his tongue was loosened by drink, he answered her questions, half flattered that she should be interested in his work, half grateful to have this one person with whom he could be honest. He survived his early, dubious years and then moved on to affluent respectability. Thereafter, Archie sometimes conveniently forgot the methods he had used and the risks he had taken in his early days.

Connie never forgot. Not even in the years after his death, when she basked in the respectability and comfort of wealth that was based impeccably on blue-chip stock-market shares. She was aware not just of the methods but of the people her husband had used in those murky early years. Most of them she had long since abandoned as they became unnecessary. She was in regular contact with none of them. But she kept the names, addresses and telephone numbers of a select few, who might be prepared to do things which were quite outside the law, provided they received appropriate remuneration. When you had fought your way up from the gutter, you kept such information as an insurance.

While Graham Reynolds and Sue Giles were conducting their uneasy reunion on the evening of November 19th, Connie Elson spent the night in agonised recollection of the man who had been buried earlier in the day. The police had not been back to her since they had come to the house on Saturday. She didn't see how they could possibly have anything more to ask her. They had probably written her off as a silly, infatuated woman, with her judgement made useless by love. Well, she was a much more resourceful woman than they thought. And perhaps they were much less clever than they thought – they didn't seem to be getting any nearer to an arrest.

At two in the morning, Connie formed a resolution. On the morning of November 20th, she called one of the men from her past at eight o'clock. He had once been her husband's chauffeur. But in the early days, he had been much more than that. He had been a bodyguard to Archie, and also what her husband had once called an "enforcer". The term came back to her now from some corner of her subconscious as she tapped out the number.

"Walter Smith. Who's that?" said a bad-tempered voice in her ear. It didn't say, "Why the hell are you disturbing me at this hour?" It was the tone of the voice which said that.

"It's Mrs Elson, Wally."

"Mrs Elson? Sorry. I was asleep, you see." A hint of apology and explanation now in the suddenly alert Birmingham voice. He knew that she only came to him with dubious propositions, but they were extremely lucrative ones. Wally liked a woman who knew the escalating price of violence and was prepared to pay it.

She paused, took a deep breath, then plunged decisively into speech. "I think I may have some more work for you, Wally. Well-paid work, of course. I'm sure you'd be interested."

Colin Pitman stood in the yard of his works, surrounded by the lorries and pantechnicons which were the basis of his wealth. This was usually where he was most at home, the world where he was comfortably in control and he and everyone around him knew it. No one tried to pull the wool over his eyes about haulage and freight, because no one, not even his longest-serving drivers, knew the business in all its facets as he did. He was a kindly man in his bluff way, aware of the home circumstances of most of the men who drove long distances for him, and willing to help them. He would adjust the schedules when a baby was due or an elderly relative was near the end. He was a comfortable autocrat within his own small empire, dispensing justice as he saw it with a discerning eye. There might be something of the Victorian master about him, but Colin Pitman accepted the best union practices and applied them.

He took care that he was outwardly his usual self on this busy Tuesday morning in Malvern, genial and gruff by turns as he saw the heavy vehicles on their different ways. But inwardly, Colin was a troubled man. He had seen Matt Walsh off on his way to Leipzig with a consignment of steel tools. It was the longest journey available that week. Normally he would have started a new man with an easier journey, but he wanted this one as far away from him and from Malvern as it was possible to be. In any case, Walsh was not a new man. He was a man who had been taken on again after being sacked. Not laid off, sacked. That had never happened before at Pitman Haulage, and his action had raised a few eyebrows in the office, because everyone had known that Walsh had been fired for fiddling his mileages; Colin had made the reasons for his action very public at the time, *pour encourager les autres.*

He thought he had carried off Walsh's reinstatement all right. Most people seemed to think he was just being particularly charitable; perhaps the boss was getting softer as he got older. But he knew, because he was no good at disguising things from himself, that he had been blackmailed. It made him uneasy, as he had never been before in this place. The smells of warm oil and diesel failed to bring the reassurance to his soul that he had hoped for when he came and stood in the yard. He wasn't sure where the notion had come from, but the thought that blackmailers always came back for more would not leave the brain of this proud, stubborn man.

He was so preoccupied with the idea that he did not notice the police car until it drew up alongside him. "Few more questions, I'm afraid," said Superintendent Lambert as he levered himself stiffly out of the front passenger seat. He smiled affably enough at the preoccupied Pitman. "You'll remember Detective Sergeant Hook. Could we go somewhere private, do you think?"

They went inside to his office, sat carefully down on the red Chesterfield which looked as if it had never been used, studied the prints of Malvern in Elgar's time, at the turn of the century, as they waited for the coffee he was determined they should have. Hook wondered if Pitman was playing for time with his insistence on the coffee. Then he decided he was too straightforward a man for that. Perhaps he just wanted to show that a man who lived in the rough world of huge machines and huge loads could offer the trappings of a cosier success.

Pitman was a man with no small talk, suspicious of their presence, and these experienced CID men did not offer him any conversational olive branches. People who were embarrassed sometimes blurted out quite revealing things.

Pitman was merely silent, and when the coffee cups were in their hands, Lambert moved straight in to the reason for their visit. "It's about the statement you made to us about what you were doing on the night of Saturday the tenth of November."

"The night when Giles was killed? Have you got any nearer to discovering who killed the bugger? I didn't like him, because of the way he treated my daughter, but—"

"Where were you on that night, Mr Pitman?"

"I told you that. I was at home."

"You don't wish to change your statement?"

"No. Why should I?"

"Because we have a signed statement from someone who says you were not at home on that night. Someone who is prepared to swear it on oath, if necessary."

"Then he's lying. Who is he?"

Lambert thought quickly, then decided that on this occasion he would reveal his source. Pitman did not strike him as a natural liar: he might well tell them the truth, if he was faced with the evidence. "I can't give you his name. He's a man you wouldn't normally consider reliable. But in this case, I think we can accept what he says, since he's confessing to a crime. He's a burglar, Mr Pitman, well known to the police. He tells us he broke into your premises on the night of Saturday the tenth of November. More precisely, and more interestingly from our point of view and yours, he tells us that there was no one in your house at eleven o'clock on that night."

"But that's impossible. The house was—" Pitman stopped abruptly, staring furiously first at his desk and then at the faces of Lambert and Hook.

They were old hands at this game. When a man was in difficulties, you didn't help him out. It was a long time before Lambert said, "You were going to say, perhaps, that your house was alarmed. That the alarm was switched on at that time. No conflict there: our man confirms that it was."

Pitman looked like a caged bear. With thick eyebrows lowered over his furious face, he gripped his desk hard with both hands, as if that were a substitute for the physical action he so desired. He said in a clipped, low voice, "You just said this – this criminal, whom you apparently think is a reliable witness, broke into my house. How could he do that if the alarm was on?"

"I said your premises, not your house, Mr Pitman. Your garage is some way from the house – perhaps you should extend your alarm system to it. Our burglar is a professional, even if a not very successful one. That's probably why you haven't yet missed anything. He took a toolbox with a set of rather expensive tools and a cordless power drill from your garage. He planned to enter the house as well, but he realised it was alarmed and that the alarm was on. According to him, there wasn't a single light showing in the house."

Colin Pitman felt more uncomfortable than he had at any time since his school days. For now, when the memory was quite useless, he remembered standing dumbly in front of a schoolmaster, caught out in some adolescent misdemeanour, squirming with no sort of reply under the master's sarcasm. He felt as exposed now as he had done then, exposed in front of a tittering classroom, moving his schoolboy weight from foot to foot. He said, trying in vain to force scorn into his voice, "Taking the word of a criminal against mine, then, are you?"

Lambert allowed himself the weary smile of a man who has listened to thirty years of lies and half-truths. "Tommy Brick's word isn't usually worth a lot, it's true. But the uniformed lads caught him red-handed on another job last night, you see. Searched his house and found the stuff from your garage among some other minor items he hadn't managed to pass on immediately. He's going to ask for four other offences to be taken into account; one of them is breaking and entering into your garage and removing the items I mentioned. We shall be asking you to identify them, in due course."

Pitman realised that he was still gripping the edge of his desk. He forced his fingers to unclench, watched the blood beginning to pulse back into the whiteness of them. He glanced up quickly at the two faces who studied him with such concentration, then folded his arms deliberately and kept his eyes resolutely upon a tiny mark on the desk in front of him. He was surprised how evenly he was able to speak when he said, "All right, I wasn't there that night. I won't try to argue."

But you did argue, thought Bert Hook. Until the evidence drove you to a point where you could argue no longer. He flicked over a new page on his notebook and said, "We shall need a full account of exactly where you were and at what times on that Saturday night, Mr Pitman."

Pitman nodded with weary acceptance, but did not look up again from the desk. "I can't give you all that. You'll see why. I was in the red-light district of Birmingham on that night. I drove around for quite some time before I committed myself. It's not a regular habit of mine, you see. I don't know the name of the streets. I don't know the name of the woman I was with. That's part of the bargain you strike with women like that, in so far as I understand it."

Lambert said, "I see. Why did you see fit to lie to us when we saw you five days ago?"

Now at last Pitman looked up at them, his eyes blazing with an astonished anger. "Think I'm proud of it, do you? Think a man wants to boast about going out and paying for it? I'd never been near a tart in my life until two years ago. But my wife's been dead and gone these five years now. And a man still has needs, you know. More's the bloody pity!" His self-contempt came pouring out in the last phrases.

Lambert did not back off. "I repeat my question. If this is true, why didn't you tell it to us last Thursday, instead of pretending you were at home on that evening? We probably wouldn't have needed to let it go any further."

"I have a daughter, Superintendent. A daughter I'm very close to. You established that when you came here the first time. She's going to find out what I've said to you today, whether I like it or not. Just as she knows that I told you I was here on Saturday night. I can't keep things from her, even when I want to."

It should have been a confession of weakness, but he said it almost proudly. Lambert said, "The tom you picked up in Birmingham. Why so far from home?"

"Because I wanted to be a long way from where anyone might know me. Anyone who might spot Colin Pitman picking up a tart!" The self-loathing again; there was a fascination with his own weakness as well as a hatred of that part of himself. "Anyway, I can be in Birmingham in less than an hour from my house."

"Was this a regular arrangement?"

"No. Of course it wasn't. Once in a while, I get lonely. Lonely and randy, if you want it all. I should have thought that much was obvious from what I've said."

"I see. It's just that if it had been a regular arrangement with the same girl, it would have made it easier for us to check your story out. We shall still have to do that, you know. A man was murdered during the hours we're speaking of, a man you told us quite openly you hated."

Pitman shrugged his huge shoulders, then allowed them to slump forward. It was as though the act of confession had exhausted him.

Hook wanted to tell him that they came across greater weaknesses and much greater evils than this. Instead, they took the details of the prostitute and the time he had spent with her. It had been drizzling with rain as he cruised the streets of the sprawling industrial city. The woman was probably in her early thirties, with longish dark hair. She had a room with a gas fire and a single bed. And a picture of the Queen on the wall above the bed, surveying the actions of this obscure subject of hers. It was the only original detail Pitman offered them. He gave the impression that once he had made his concession to the persistent demands of his loins, he hadn't noticed a great deal about his partner or her surroundings while taking his dubious pleasure.

Perhaps he hadn't, but it wouldn't make it easy to find the woman who might give him an alibi for that November night.

When they had gone, Colin Pitman sat and looked at the wall for a long time. He didn't trust the police to keep the secret of what he had just told them. Even if they tried, it would have to come out sooner or later, as they tested one person's story against another. It was a murder investigation, as they kept reminding him. He picked up the phone, made sure that he had an outside line, that no one in the outer office was listening. The phone rang so long that he thought Sue was not in. Then, just when he was wondering why she had not put the answerphone on, his daughter picked up the phone. She must have come from a distance; he could hear her breathlessness as she gave her name.

He said tersely, "It's Dad, Sue. The police have been here again. They've rumbled that I wasn't here on that Saturday night. You'd better hear what I've had to tell them."

*   *   *

The notice over the bed said in red capital letters NIL BY MOUTH. As if she were an animal, not able to speak for herself, thought John Lambert. The letters seemed to grow larger as he sat by the bed, until they vibrated with a life of their own, depriving him of the power of speech and the ability to think rationally.

"There's plenty of bread in the freezer," said Christine, desperately terminating a long pause, "but don't you go living on just toast, the way you tend to do. There's plenty of ham and cheese in the fridge, and I bought half a dozen of those complete meals for one." She looked down at his long hand laid on top of her small one on the blankets. Both of them had wanted some intimacy at this last meeting before her operation, but neither of them was easy with even this small gesture, with other people around. She felt that all the other women in the ward must be watching this new arrival, studying her relationship with the man whom some of them probably knew: Superintendent Lambert was by now something of a local celebrity, and the young nurse had asked her loudly as she took away her suitcase of clothes whether she was the wife of *the* Mr Lambert.

He said, "I expect I shall have Caroline and Jacky fussing round me, as though I was helpless!" He remembered vividly that he had mouthed all these clichés last time she had been here for surgery, when she had had the mastectomy. Why was memory so selective, throwing up in stark detail all the trivial things which merely left you embarrassed, but failing to recall all the deep, philosophical things he had thought of to say at this time?

He wanted to say it had been a good marriage, that he

was glad they hadn't separated in those early years when it had seemed that his job and his fierce preoccupation with it might divide them. But that would seem like an epitaph, would sound as if he didn't expect that she would come out of this alive. He sought desperately for something to say, could only come up with the thought that nurses, like policemen, looked younger with each passing year.

Christine studied the lined, anxious face with its troubled grey eyes. She felt a searing sympathy for this normally so articulate man, which she supposed must be love. She said, "How's the case going? Have you found out who killed our schoolteacher yet?"

"No. He doesn't seem to have been quite your usual schoolteacher. Whatever that might be!" He found guiltily that he wanted to talk about the case. His brain felt freed with her question, began to work almost normally again. "He had been involved with at least three women; two of them loved him – the third one, who didn't, was once his wife."

Christine grinned. "It was probably the wife who did it. You always said they're the likeliest candidates. There were one or two occasions when I might have done you in, if you'd only been there at the time."

He grinned back, gave a little squeeze to the hand he was surprised to find still beneath his. "This wife seems to have been in the clear, though. She was in Ireland at the time. We've had the Irish police check it out for us."

"One of the other two women, then?"

"Perhaps. We haven't been able to clear either of them, as yet. We're not being sexist about it: there are a couple of men in the frame as well." Three, if you include that health hazard Aubrey Bass, he thought. He somehow couldn't see Aubrey as a killer.

"Hope it comes right for you, John." She answered his squeeze. And in that moment a thought came to him which had escaped him until now, when it should have been obvious. He stood up, awkwardly relinquishing her hand. "Better be on my way, I suppose. Before they come and throw me out." He looked hopefully for the advent of a stern sister, but there was no sign.

It was as usual Christine who had to help him out. "Off you go, then. Give me a chance of a rest and a read. I've been looking forward to that."

He embraced her clumsily, feeling that they were the centre of attention for the whole ward, though it was not so. "It'll be all right, you know!" she whispered in his ear.

"Of course it will! You're a tough little bugger you are, underneath!" he said. Underneath what, he thought.

They left it like that, each pretending not to harbour the thought that this might be the last they saw of each other, each pretending that this profoundly serious moment was really rather trivial. They waved at each other shyly as he reached the exit.

It was another milestone reached in life's dark comedy.

Fourteen

J ob titles have become more high-flown with each
passing year. Where the dustbinmen would once spot
a rat and send for the rat-catcher, the refuse disposal
operatives now report the matter to their senior deploy-
ment officer, who may, if the latest cuts have left such
services unimpaired, sanction the utilisation of the council rodent operatives.

Occasionally, a new title is well justified. Zoe Ross,
who a decade earlier might have been called a secretary, was now Personal Assistant to the Chief Execu-
tive. It was an accurate description of her role in the
firm, for the man she assisted would certainly have
been lost without her. She did far more than type, and
occasionally improve, his letters. She discussed his
week's schedule, arranged his appointments, booked
his first-class tickets for his monthly flights across the
Atlantic, diverted people who wanted to see him to
other and more appropriate executives of the firm. She
was an integral part of her boss's success, and he was
shrewd enough to realise it. He even tried to ensure
that her holidays coincided with his. On one occasion,
though he admitted it to no one, he had hastily rear-

173

ranged his family fortnight in Tuscany to coincide with Zoe's choice of break.

On the morning of Wednesday, November 21st, Zoe was her usual efficient self. She put through a call to Zurich to question the interest on the loan that was financing a Swiss development, briefed her man on the background of a raw materials supplier who was coming to see him in the afternoon, contacted the chef to discuss the menu for the board lunch on the morrow, and cancelled a booking on the British Airways shuttle to Glasgow in the following week which was now no longer necessary. She was contemplating a well-earned coffee when the personal call came through to her.

It was a man's voice, harsh but indistinct – the speaker had put a pair of tights over the phone, but Zoe had no knowledge of such contrivances. It said, "You had better listen carefully, Ms Ross. I know all about the murder of Ted Giles. I know all about your part in it."

She said, trying to use her most official and neutral voice, "Who is that? I had no part in Ted's murder. If you're trying to threaten me, you ought to know that—"

"Don't talk, listen. You don't have a choice. Be at the Hare and Hounds hotel on the A438 tonight. You know it?"

"I think so. Between Ledbury and Hereford? But—"

"That's it. Be there at seven thirty."

"Look, if you think I'm going to go out there without even knowing who I'm meeting or what this is about, you're very much—"

"You don't have a choice. Seven thirty. Don't be late."

The voice had spoken throughout in a harsh, unemotional monotone. It was that unwavering, muffled tone which made it so chilling, Zoe thought. She dialled 1471, but the altogether more pleasant voice there told her that the caller had withheld their number.

She wasn't walking into that one, she told herself for the rest of the day. She wasn't going to be silly enough to go out to an assignation with an unknown man at night. Whatever that odious speaker might know about the way Ted had been killed.

John Lambert knew that the best way to shut out the thoughts of his wife under the surgeon's knife was to concentrate on his work. He was a little disconcerted by how easily that concentration came to him, once he was in his morning conference with DI Rushton and DS Hook.

Somewhere at the back of the Superintendent's mind there was a solution to this case. He had made sense of another piece of it as he talked with Christine in the hospital last night, but as he had tossed through an almost sleepless night in his lonely bed, he had been unable to fit this piece into a pattern of the whole case. The connections which might draw the various sections together into a picture were still absent. He was glad to have the tangible distraction of this meeting and the scraps of new evidence it would offer him.

Chris Rushton, looking as spruce and alert as always in the morning, was full of the small triumph he had engineered. Trying hard to look modest, and in Bert Hook's view succeeding only in looking like a duck preening its feathers, he said, "I arranged for surveillance

on our malodorous friend Aubrey Bass when he left us."
Lambert knew that, for he had had to sanction the
overtime, but he didn't interrupt his Inspector. "Well,
it paid off. I never believed Bass's tale that he knew
nothing about the use of his van. Even if he wasn't
directly involved himself, I reckon he knew his van
was being used to move that body. He went straight
back to his flat from here when we released him. And
within half an hour, he was visited by Zoe Ross."

He was like a conjurer producing a rabbit from an
immaculate black top hat. It was Bert Hook, willing to be
impressed, but wanting to know exactly what they had
acquired through Rushton's initiative, who asked,
"Why?"

Lambert stepped in, taking responsibility. "We don't
know, as yet. Bass has given us nothing worthwhile
about it – he told Chris last night that she just wanted
to know about his van and how far we'd got towards the
truth – and I've told Chris not to approach Zoe Ross as
yet. I don't think anyone else is likely to be killed and I'd
like to know just what she's up to. We've transferred the
surveillance from Bass to her. We'll give it another day; if
she's done nothing very revealing by then, we'll have to
see her and find out just what she was up to when she met
Aubrey Bass."

Rushton said, "I've done some digging into the backgrounds of our suspects, as you asked me to, John." It
was an embarrassment for him to use his chief's first
name, as Lambert demanded, and he actually blushed as
he forced himself to do it now. Hook was much amused:
blushing was a phenomenon not common among police-

men, and surely unique among detective inspectors. "None of them has a record, as you might expect, but they've all lived in the area for at least ten years, so the boys on the ground have been able to piece together quite a lot. Some of it's no more than gossip or rumour, so I couldn't say how reliable it is."

"Let's have it, then. Take the men first, on this occasion."

"Right. Colin Pitman. Yorkshireman. But been in this area for over thirty years. Originally a motor mechanic. Bought his own lorry, built up a prosperous business from scratch. Blunt and direct, but people say he's a fair man. Everyone seems to think that; it's unusual, in the case of a successful businessman – usually he has enemies, if it's only from jealousy. Even the man he bought out of the yard he operates from in Malvern thinks he's Honest Colin."

"And yet he lied to us. At least once, and maybe twice, for all we know as yet. No trace of the tom he picked up on that Saturday night, is there, Chris?"

"None yet. Perhaps never will be. Finding the right hooker in Birmingham is looking for a needle in a haystack."

"Anyway, we now know he lied to us the first time, when he said he'd been at home that night. What could have made an honest man do that?"

"Unnerved when he found himself involved in a murder inquiry?" suggested Hook. They had seen that often enough: people who were perfectly innocent but who found themselves without an alibi tended to panic and invent one for themselves.

"Pitman didn't seem the type to lose his nerve, if he had nothing to hide," said Lambert, "though he's certainly old fashioned enough to be ashamed about resorting to prostitutes and apprehensive about being humiliated if all was revealed."

"Especially if his daughter were to find out," said Hook. "He dotes on her and doesn't trouble to disguise it."

Lambert nodded. "Ironic that it should take a burglar to expose a normally honest man. Where is Tommy Brick at the moment, Chris?"

Rushton tapped out an entry into a computer file. "He was bailed to appear at the Crown Court next month. He's pleading guilty and asking now for five other offences to be taken into account – one of them theft from Colin Pitman's garage."

"I might have a word with him about his activities at Pitman's house today or tomorrow. What about Graham Reynolds?"

"We've been able to firm up his motive. He's planning to marry Sue Giles and wed himself to a fortune. She's affluent enough already – her mother left her money – and must have high expectations from her doting father: she's the only child. Ted Giles was being sticky about the divorce, but he couldn't have held out for ever. Of course, he'd have come out of it with a handsome settlement – perhaps that is what he was really holding out for. Sue Giles might well have had to sell that beautiful house of hers to pay him off. All that is now preserved for the new husband."

Hook said, "But we knew about that the day after the murder. You said you'd found something new."

"We have. Graham Reynolds is a successful teacher. Most of the parents think well of him. But he's a bit fond of the gee-gees. The wrong ones, it seems, when it comes to picking winners. He's seven thousand in debt, and being pressed to settle. It wouldn't do him any good in the educational profession, if that came out. It's quite convenient for him that he won't have to wait for a long lawyers' wrangle over the Gileses' divorce, apart from the money this death has preserved for him."

Lambert shrugged. "Motive's all very well, but what about opportunity?"

"That's the snag. There seems no doubt he was in Ireland with Sue Giles on the night of the murder. Booked into adjoining rooms with a connecting door. We've had the Gardi check it out. That lets both of them out."

"Very neatly. It doesn't prevent them employing someone else to do the dirty work while they sat on the shores of Lake Killarney with a cast-iron alibi," Hook pointed out. He hadn't particularly liked either Ted Giles's widow or the man she planned to marry; if this crime had to be down to one of the five or six people they were investigating, he would have preferred it to be one of them.

"That's perfectly true, of course," said Rushton, "but it's equally true that any one of our suspects could have used a contract killer to get rid of Giles. Some of them are more likely to have the right contacts than others. In that respect, Constance Elson looks interesting. She's a pillar of bourgeois respectability now; she pays her taxes and supports her charities. But it was her husband who made

179

the fortune, and he seems to have used some pretty dubious methods in his early days. His employees were twice involved in GBH cases. There was a prosecution planned for one of them on a demanding money with menaces charge in Birmingham, twenty-three years ago; the CPS eventually dropped it on the grounds of lack of evidence. The same thing happened a year or so later when they tried to get Archie Elson himself for fraud. Connie was married to him then – she'd be about twenty-three or twenty-four, I think. She may not have known much about what he was up to – wives often don't, as we know. And Archie Elson was straight for a good fifteen years before he died. But I suppose it's just possible that his widow retained one or two links with that murky past."

Lambert nodded, thinking of the intense woman he had interviewed rather than the one Hook had reported weeping at the funeral. "She was certainly very much infatuated with Ted Giles. She thought he was going to marry her when he was eventually divorced, but I believe he had other plans altogether. If she had rumbled him, she might well have been jealous enough to want him dead. She could have killed him herself, of course. We've known from the outset that a woman could certainly have drawn that wire around Giles's neck – no great strength needed, once he was surprised by someone behind him."

Rushton nodded. "That applies to Zoe Ross as well. She seems to have been equally taken with Ted Giles. She's a highly competent young woman – her firm is very anxious to keep her, apparently. I can't see her taking

180

kindly to any deception or rejection from Giles. It will be interesting to hear what she has to say about her connection with Aubrey Bass: forensic are quite certain now that his van was used for the disposal of the body."

The three of them broke up then. Lambert looked at his watch as soon as he was alone. Too early to ring the hospital yet. Something was again nagging at his mind about this case though; he was sure there were more details somewhere that he had not yet weighted with their full importance.

Ten minutes later, he picked up the phone. "Get me a call through to the Garda station in Killarney," he said.

At two thirty, there was still no news from the hospital. "Mrs Lambert is still down in theatre," said the ward sister's voice with practised, professional neutrality. "I don't think we shall have anything to tell you for some time yet."

It was that kind of day, it seemed. The man Lambert needed in Killarney was off duty all day; they would ring back in the morning. Hook, looking at the long, lined face, decided that the only way to distract the chief during this limbo in both his professional and private lives was to make the ultimate sacrifice. He swallowed hard and made the plunge, forcing the lie he knew would be swallowed eagerly. "If there's nothing more we can do here for the time being, we could steal an hour and you could give me a golf lesson," he said with a sickly smile.

Bert knew the weather could not save him. It was a day of hard blue sky and little cloud. There would be a frost before the night was over, but it was a pleasant autumn

181

day, dry and crisp in the hour before the early twilight.

"Get your feet and shoulders lined up with these," said Lambert. He set two of Bert's clubs on parallel lines at his feet. "Imagine they're railway lines and you're going to send your ball away along them, straight and true."

Bert tried. The ball sliced away to the right. "Aaaah!" said Lambert with deep satisfaction. Hook thought Archimedes had probably made that noise, immediately before "Eureka". Lambert said, "Everyone does that!" as if that might be some sort of consolation. "You've lined your feet up straight, but not your shoulders. Shoulders are the difficult part."

They would be, thought Hook. Lambert twisted his torso until the offending items were on the line he wanted. Bert found that he could no longer see the ball.

"You can drop your right shoulder a little, if you like," said Lambert, as though offering a special treat. Then, as Hook was ready to hit the next ball, he yelled, "But for goodness" sake keep your left arm straight! That should be built into your swing by now – I shouldn't need to tell you that."

Bert considered giving his teacher the look of smouldering contempt he had reserved for favoured batsmen in his cricketing days. But he was a patient man; he reminded himself that the chief was under stress, that this exercise was meant to be therapy for him. Quite what it would be for Bert was another matter. He dispatched his next shot with an awful sense of déjà vu. It was a horrid top, stinging his fingers on that cold afternoon.

"Your HEAD moved!" said Lambert triumphantly.

'Course it bloody did, thought Hook. After you'd

moved me into that Quasimodo stance, it was either that or a broken neck. He said brightly, "Yes, it did, John. I felt it go myself."

"Well, then, you know what to do," said Lambert sternly. There followed a rapid series of adjustments, after each of which Hook continued to produce the offending slice. Lambert moved the ball back in Bert's stance, then forward in a revised stance. He moved his right shoulder up, then down. He moved his right knee in, then out. He'll have me doing the Hokey-kokey before he lets me go, thought Hook desperately. Another ball rolled away into the long grass beneath the trees on the right of the practice ground. He perceived a dim hope: he might eventually run out of practice balls.

"Oh dear, oh dear!" sighed Lambert. "You're gripping the club like a rheumatic limpet. For goodness' sake loosen up! Grip it as if it is an injured bird you're caressing. Or as lightly as if you were handling your own—"

"All right, I've got the message!" snarled Hook. Therapy, he said to himself. Therapy. The man needs this diversion. Therapy: that's why you're here.

A moment later, his 5-iron, held now with the tenderest of loving care, flew from his grasp and landed twenty yards away in light mud. Hook, detaching himself from the balletic follow-through on which his mentor had insisted, set off at a trot after the errant club. "Losing my footing!" he called over his shoulder. "Balls all gone!" he added when he reached the 5-iron. He picked it up nimbly, his ample frame scarcely breaking stride as he moved away from Lambert. "Enough for today!" he shouted, as he put more distance between him and his fount of golfing knowledge. He did not slow to a walk until he reached the safety of the car park.

Lambert reflected that for a man in the final stages of an Open University degree, Bert Hook was not very articulate. Still, no doubt he was grateful for an old hand's time and patience on the practice ground.

Zoe Ross drove even more slowly once she reached the A438. She did not want to get to the Hare and Hounds, perhaps to hear clearly that sinister muffled voice which had used the phone to summon her to the place. In the daylight, she had been able to laugh away her fears. Now, on this cold, clear but moonless night, this journey seemed foolhardy in the extreme.

Yet she felt like the rabbit hypnotised by the stoat. The man seemed to know something about how Ted had died, and the police didn't seem to be getting anywhere, as far as she could tell. If they had that oaf Aubrey Bass in the frame for it, they couldn't be very near to finding the real murderer. She shivered at that word, despite the warmth in her hard-top MG.

When the cheerful orange lights of the old pub appeared out of the darkness, she was frightened, not relieved. She had planned to park in front of it, where she could see and be seen, but she realised now that the building's front was almost on the road, that the only safe parking was in the area the sign indicated at the rear. She almost accelerated away and drove on. Yet she knew that even if she did that, she would return. She could not face a long night and the working hours of the next day waiting for that muffled voice to renew its contact with her.

She had hoped that the car park at the rear of the pub would be illuminated. It was not. After the brightness of the frontage, the inky blackness here was the more marked. Her headlights threw up only two other cars, at the far end of the gravelled yard. Seven thirty was a quiet time, after the people who called in for a drink on their way home from work had gone, before most of the evening drinkers had arrived. She wondered as she switched off her headlights whether the time had been chosen for that reason.

The man she was meeting must already be inside the old inn. She had hesitated for so long that she was now ten minutes late. She thought she would look at his car before she went in. She might even take the number, in case he was as unpleasant as he sounded on the phone. She wasn't used to being spoken to like that, and she didn't like it. And she hadn't yet found out how much he knew about Ted's death.

The cold hit her as soon as she slid her legs out of the car. Perhaps she should have worn trousers for this, but she had had no time to change after work. She heard a single footstep, but before she was fully upright from the low car the scarf was round her neck and the bag was over her head.

From being a child, she had felt a terror of having her head covered, a blind panic even when joking friends threw a coat over it. She felt that if she couldn't see, then in a few moments she wouldn't be able to hear, and immediately after that she wouldn't be able to breathe.

She had always lashed out and screamed in those childish days, furious beyond all reason at the laughing children around her who had reduced her to such weakness.

Now it seemed as if all those past episodes had been a preparation for her real death, here in this profound darkness, at the hands of this anonymous assailant who neither laughed nor spoke. She threw her hands out behind her, grasped the powerful forearms which held her captive, but was easily shaken off. The scarf tightened round her throat, crushing her breath as it rose to her throat to scream, stifling her feeble resistance.

And then, when she thought it could get no worse, he began to hit her. Systematically, with the back of his strong hands, again and again, across her face beneath the bag. She felt her nose go, felt the salt blood which had been pounding in her ears running now into her mouth, raised her hands to try to protect her eyes. As she lost consciousness, she prayed that death would be quick, that she wouldn't fight as she stifled beneath this awful bag, in case that would mean that these blows went on. Her last, ridiculous hope was that he wouldn't make too horrible a mess of her face, because that would upset her mother when she saw her in the coffin.

The man stopped hitting her when he felt the body relax. There was no need to risk a murder rap, however remote the chances of discovery might be. He laid the slender frame down carefully, almost tenderly, beside the new MG, then drove swiftly away.

Fifteen

For a moment Lambert was puzzled by the bird screaming into his dream. Then he realised that it was the phone shrilling beside the bed.

"How is she?" It was Hook, presuming on long acquaintance to ring before eight in the morning.

"Christine's fine. Well, *they* said fine: I suppose all that means is that she's come through the surgery. She was still unconscious when I went in last night; they had her in a room on her own at the end of the ward. She had tubes and drips and electric monitors all around her. But they said that's normal after major heart surgery."

"That's really good news, John. Eleanor will be delighted. I don't suppose you got much sleep last night."

"As a matter of fact, I slept very well. I was still asleep when you rang." He suddenly felt very guilty. "I must be an insensitive sod."

"Relief, that's all it would be. Not surprising, either . . . Well, I'll leave you to get on with it – just wanted to know how she was, that's all."

It was Hook's hesitations which made his chief say sharply, "Something's happened, hasn't it? Is it something to do with the Giles case?"

"Well, yes, but you don't need to worry about it. You've got quite enough to—"

"Come on, Bert. What is it?"

"Zoe Ross. She was attacked last night. In the car park of the Hare and Hounds, out on the Ledbury–Hereford road."

"How badly is she hurt?"

"We don't have a full report yet. She's unconscious, but we've got a WPC at her bedside. The hospital said the injuries were nasty, but not life-threatening. She's in Hereford General."

Where Christine was. Perhaps she had even been brought in whilst he was there last night. He said dully, "I thought Zoe Ross was supposed to be under surveillance."

"Our man followed her car in his. When she drove into the pub car park, he waited five minutes before he followed her." It was standard procedure. Wait to see if she drove straight out again. Once it was safe to assume she had gone into the pub, follow her after a safe interval, so that she would not suspect that she was being followed.

"You say she was attacked in the car park. Who found her?"

"Our bloke did. He was just turning in to the Hare and Hounds when a car came out past him and drove away quickly. It's a narrow entry and he was too close to the car to get its number at the front, I'm afraid. He thinks the bulb over the rear number plate wasn't on. A black or a dark blue Escort Ghia, he says."

"Common as muck. Probably stolen. And probably

dumped last night." Lambert didn't trouble to disguise his disgust.

"Yes. DC Cox knows that. If it happened as he says, there isn't a lot he could have done about it." Hook, as usual, was prepared to give a young officer the benefit of the doubt. "He found the girl he had been tailing unconscious beside her own MG. It looks as though the bastard in the Escort threw a bag over Zoe Ross's head as she got out of the low seat and then beat her systematically about the head. As yet, we have no idea why."

Lambert looked at his watch. It was two minutes to eight. "I'll be in CID in an hour, Bert. I've a call to make on the way in, but it won't take long."

He rang the hospital, got the morning bulletin from the ward sister who had taken over at six. Mrs Christine Lambert was conscious, had taken a little liquid – had drunk most of a cup of hospital tea, actually, so she must be recovering! He might see her later that morning if he wished, just for a few minutes, but she wasn't to be overtaxed at this stage.

Lambert said he would be there between eleven and twelve. He tried not to think how conveniently that would suit his schedule for the day, now that there was that other patient he wanted to see in Hereford General Hospital.

Tommy Brick, the burglar who had admitted to breaking and entering Colin Pitman's garage on the night of Saturday, November 10th, was a sharp-featured whippet of a man. His small and wiry body might have been designed for squeezing through small spaces. Tommy, who was now over fifty, with a sallow skin and thinning grey hair, had in his time squeezed through a good few pantry and toilet windows which householders had thought too small for the human frame.

But now he had pleaded guilty to five burglaries. When he opened the paint-blistered door of his house in Gloucester and peered blearily at Lambert's identification, he had the downcast look of a defeated old pro. "What do *you* want?" he said ill-humouredly. "You know I've held up my hand and I'm going to the Quarter Sessions. This is 'arrassment, this is."

Lambert grinned and nodded. He looked at the four-inch gap which is all that Brick had permitted him when he opened the door. "It might well turn into persecution if you don't let me in, Tommy. Ruin your reputation, won't it, if you're seen with a Superintendent on your doorstep?"

It was a persuasive argument. Brick opened the door, looked suspiciously up and down the short, empty street of mean Victorian houses, and turned back into the house. He wore a vest and striped pyjama trousers. He had never owned a dressing gown, and as his slippers shuffled away from Lambert, the split in the seat of his pyjamas revealed thin buttocks, which winked alarmingly away from the policeman and into the living room. Tommy switched on the single bar of an electric fire and crouched over it. He repeated, as if it were the recurring chorus of his song of protest. "This is 'arrassment, this is. I already made a statement for that poncy bugger Rushton."

"Of course you did, Tommy. I read it with interest.

Quite an interesting document, with the details of your different activities. But as it happens, it doesn't contain all the information I need. You're in a position to help us with our enquiries into another case, you see. It's fair to say that Tommy Brick has never been quite so important."

"I'm not grassing on anybody. Tommy Brick ain't no grass. You can 'arrass me all you like but I won't grass." His mouth set into the sullen refusal of a child.

And indeed the simple code of small criminals was not unlike the schoolboy reluctance to snitch on classmates, thought Lambert. He said calmly, "You'll talk to me about this one, Tommy. Someone's going to get a murder rap at the end of it."

A sharp intake of breath between the long rabbit teeth, a widening of the rheumy grey eyes. Despite himself, Tommy was impressed by a crime that was way beyond his experience and aspirations. "I thought it were funny, a superintendent coming after *me*," he said. Whatever his declared and automatic hatred of the pigs, there was something very near to pride in his voice. He had the attention of a very big pig indeed. And with the mention of murder, they both knew that he was going to talk; he was way out of his league here, and playing away.

Lambert took him through the half-hour he had spent in that Saturday night darkness around the big, stone-built house of Colin Pitman. Within minutes, Brick, rubbing his hands to spread the warmth from the electric fire and leaning towards this opponent from the other side of the law, was speaking like a confidant. "People spend fortunes getting their houses alarmed, then forget all about their garages. There can be a lot of valuable stuff in garages, these days. Course, the garage at that place was well away from the house – I reckon it's what used to be the stables, in the old days. But that's all the more reason for having it alarmed. You could do that garage over even if there was someone at home."

"Which there wasn't, on that Saturday night when you were there."

"No."

"You're sure of that?"

"Course I am." He looked offended for a moment, as though his professional expertise had been questioned. "I went all round the place, and there wasn't a light showing anywhere. Not even the light of a television. And the curtains was open, so I could see. There was some nice stuff in there, but I could see the alarm was on. It's one of the latest electronic ones, wired directly through to the station, I should think. Some places you can rely on twenty minutes before your lot show, but at Pitman's house in Malvern, the local cop shop's just round the corner."

"You're sure the curtains were open, even in the living rooms?"

"Everywhere. Even in the downstairs khazi." This was apparently the height of impropriety, for a person of Brick's delicate sensibilities.

Lambert took him through the items he had taken from the garage. The little man looked shifty again: perhaps he had taken other small items, beyond those found in this house when the police searched it, and had disposed of those before his persecutors caught up with him. But that did not concern Lambert. He simply wanted to know whether a single, larger item had been in the garage when Brick had forced the side door and entered it.

It had. Tommy Brick had fancied stealing it with the rest of his booty. But the removal of it had been beyond him, he said regretfully. Lambert had the answer he had expected.

Superintendent Lambert arrived in the Murder Room in the Oldford CID section ten minutes later than the nine o'clock he had forecast. He found the place filled with a quiet excitement, most of which radiated from the immaculate figure of DI Rushton.

"We've found the Escort Ghia used in the attack on Zoe Ross last night."

"We?"

"Well, uniform found it, actually. It was dumped in Ross-on-Wye last night. Down by the river, to the south of the town."

"Fingerprint boys on it now?"

"Yes."

"They won't find anything." Lambert felt an unworthy need to deflate the spruce and self-satisfied young Inspector. "If the man was a professional, as he probably was, he'd be wearing gloves from the moment he took the car to the moment he dumped it."

"I expect he did. But we've had a stroke of luck. One of our doughty Herefordshire citizens did his duty. He was on his way to his local, the Wilton Arms, when he saw this fellow leave the car. He didn't lock it, which is what caught our witness's attention. Then he walked to the Wilton Arms himself, closely followed by our curious civilian."

"Perhaps he wasn't such a professional, after all." The first move after you'd dumped a car was usually to get the hell out of the area, as fast as you could.

"Or perhaps he was just ultra-cool. He'd got rid of the car, only a few miles from where he'd attacked Zoe. When he left it at the roadside with the keys in, there was a fair chance that it would be stolen again. It was only eight o'clock on a dark November night when he left it there."

Or perhaps, thought Lambert, he was so excited by the punishment he had just inflicted on a helpless woman that he was on a high, wanting a drink to celebrate and feeling invincible at the same time. Violence often had the effect of a drug on those who used it: it was that effect as much as the financial rewards which made some people choose to live by it. Whatever the reason for his conduct, the fact that he had been observed by a dutiful bystander was a bonus for the police. "So what happened in the pub?"

"He had a pint and a whisky chaser. Then another whisky: perhaps a double, but our man isn't sure. All downed within about fifteen minutes. Then he rang for a taxi, and left when it arrived."

"You're going to tell me our witness heard him ask the driver for an address."

Rushton smiled. "No. All good things come to an end, I'm afraid. Except in fairy tales. Our man stayed in the pub when his quarry left. But we're checking with the publican: he might know the taxi firm which was used. If he does, we can soon find the driver and quiz him."

"When did our witness come forward?"

"Last night. When he left the pub, he walked back past the black Escort and saw the keys were still in it. So he extracted them, took them into the police station at Ross, and reported a suspected stolen vehicle and what I've just told you about it. Unfortunately, it wasn't until I came in this morning and got DC Cox's account of the attack on Zoe Ross that the two were connected. I've had our witness brought into the station. Got him out of bed, in fact; he's been here about twenty minutes. He's a retired civil servant. He reckons he got a very good full-face view of our car-dumper in good light, at the bar of the Wilton Arms. No more than four yards away, he says, and there weren't many other people around: Wednesday's a quiet night, and it was still only just after eight o'clock."

"So where is he now?"

"In an interview room. We've shut him away with the books of mug shots of men with GBH records."

"Good work, Chris. Back to our murder for a moment. We still don't have an exact location established, do we?"

"No. Only negatives. Jack Johnson and his SOC team checked out Ted Giles's flat carefully: they're pretty sure he didn't die there. Forensic are quite certain that Aubrey Bass's van was used to dump the body, but they don't think he died in the vehicle – there's no evidence of any struggle. Jack Johnson went and had a look round the spot where Bass says it was parked on that Saturday, but he didn't find anything."

Lambert nodded. "Get Jack and his boys to have a look around the rear exit of the flats to the car park. There might have been a bulb off there on that Saturday night: the porter was replacing one when we went round to Giles's flat on the Tuesday. That would have made it conveniently dark for anyone taking Giles by surprise as he came out. He was supposed to be visiting Zoe Ross that night, according to what she told us."

The switchboard came through at that moment with a call for Superintendent Lambert from the Irish Garda station in Killarney. The PC who had given them the information about Sue Giles's and Graham Reynolds' stay at the Lakeside Hotel was back on duty. Lambert outlined the questions he wanted asked to the Inspector: protocol wouldn't allow him to speak to a junior officer in another country's force directly. "Leave it with me," said a rich Irish voice.

In five minutes, Inspector O'Connell was back on the line. "You'd better speak to him yourself," he said grimly.

Lambert could tell from the subdued tone of the thick Irish brogue that a severe bollocking had been administered. He suspected he knew why, and when he had asked the young officer his questions about the weekend of November 10th, he knew he was right. Another piece in the picture. It was complete enough now for him to make his move.

After the noise and bustle of the CID section, the hospital seemed very quiet in the late morning of a still November day.

The small figure in the bed still looked very vulnerable,

as though it was kept going only by the mass of medical technology which surrounded it. He sat down gingerly on the straight chair beside the bed; he felt as though his very presence might upset the delicate machinery, if he did not move with extreme care. But he must have made some small sound, for the head he had thought unconscious turned towards him and smiled. The mouth said softly, "I'm still here, you see . . . I told you I was a tough old bugger! . . . I'm glad it's over, though. I expect you are, too."

When the mouth spoke, it became Christine's mouth again, instead of the atrophied lips of someone very ill and beyond his help. But her voice was deep and hoarse. He said, "Yes. Is it very . . ." He gestured helplessly towards her chest, an articulate man suddenly bereft of the power of speech.

She turned her face towards him, became his wife again, alive, struggling for breath a little, but miraculously articulate. "It's a bit painful, yes, at the moment. As though someone's dumped a heavy weight on it. But that's to be expected, they say. Should ease in a few days." Her brow puckered as she tried to ease her position and sent a dagger of pain shooting through the small torso under the blankets.

"Shall I get a nurse?" said Lambert, preparing to panic, half-rising from his seat. The line pulsing across the green screen behind his wife didn't seem to have speeded up its soft bleeping; he wished he knew what on earth it signified.

"Certainly not. If I can't even grimace without you sounding the alarm, you'd better go."

He smiled with her at his own foolishness. "I'll have to go soon, anyway. The Sister said I was only to come in for a few minutes." Guilt that he should be so relieved about that surged through him and with infinite care, he gathered the small hand on top of the bedclothes between his two larger ones. It was reassuringly warm. Christine was still in the special care room at the end of the ward; he looked through into the larger world of the ward beyond her open door, saw the vases filled with colour, and said, "I didn't bring you any flowers."

"Last thing I want, at present. I've only just stopped sicking up the anaesthetic. At least, I hope I've stopped. Hurts me a bit when I do that, I can tell you."

He let go of her hand and stood up, an awkward, shambling figure, wondering how to take his leave of his own wife, when it should have been easy and spontaneous. "Better be on my way. Don't want them coming in to throw me out. The girls send their love – they'll be in to see you later, as soon as I give them the go-ahead."

"You can bring me some fruit in a day or two. Then you can sit and eat it. It will give you something to do when you're visiting." Her speech was slow, but she grinned up at him with a flash of her old spirit. He bent and kissed her swiftly on her forehead: the skin felt very warm and dry when his lips brushed it. He looked back when he got to the door of the room, but her eyes had shut in exhaustion and it seemed that she was already asleep.

The Sister looked up from her papers and said with a quick smile, "She's going to be all right, you know. We have people in here much older than her who make perfectly good recoveries from heart surgery." He decided he must look very anxious: everyone seemed bent on reassuring him about Christine today. As if he had ever had any doubts about it.

He became Superintendent Lambert again when he asked her for directions to the ward where Zoe Ross lay. He found her easily enough, guided by the figure of the policewoman who sat patiently reading a magazine just outside the door of the ward. A police presence nowadays is kept low-key and as far as possible invisible to other patients.

He listened to her report, found that she hadn't yet been allowed in to speak to the recovering Ms Ross, and sought out the Ward Sister. She was a stocky fifty-year-old of the old school of nursing, trained in the days of porcclain bedpans and visiting hours strictly limited to an hour a day. "I'm afraid she mustn't be disturbed yet," this formidable figure in blue told him. "Perhaps this evening, if she continues without setbacks. Whatever she's done, Superintendent, she remains a patient while she's in my care, and I shall treat her accordingly."

Lambert smiled. "She hasn't *done* anything, Sister. She's a victim, not a criminal. I only want five minutes with her. We're trying to find out who did this to her, and she may be able to help me."

He saw her resolution weakening. But she did not relinquish the field to him without an assertion of her rights. "As you say it's so important, I'll go and see for myself whether she is fit to talk to you for a few minutes. But you will have to abide by my decision."

While she was checking her patient, he made a phone

call from her room to Rushton in the CID section. The DI told him with satisfaction that his retired civil servant had picked out a face which he thought belonged to the man he had seen in the Wilton Arms on the previous evening. "It's a man who goes by the name of Walter Smith, among several others. Started as a heavy with a night-club operator now in prison, for supplying drugs in his clubs. Wally Smith is now a freelance, specialising in contract violence. Contract killing, they think in Birmingham, but that's never been pinned on him. All he's got is three years for GBH at the end of the eighties. Sounds like our man."

"Sounds very like our man," said Lambert. He saw the sister nodding at him through the glass. "I'm about to speak to Zoe Ross now. I'll get what I can from her and see you later."

He could see from her eyes that she recognised him. He was not sure that he would have recognised her. Her nose had obviously been broken and reset; it was grotesquely swollen and discoloured. It looked like an overripe beetroot – as if blood would well out of it if you merely touched it. She had scores of tiny butterfly stitches in the torn skin of the upper part of her face and around the line of her jaw; the pupils of her eyes peered out from blackened circles.

But curiously, her mouth and lips seemed almost unharmed. They smiled at him and said, "The nurse says I look like a bad-tempered panda. She won't let me have a mirror."

"Very wise," he said. "But you'll look a lot better in a day or two. Facial injuries are among the quickest to mend."

"You speak like an expert. I suppose you see a lot of bad injuries."

"More than I want to. Used to see a lot more, years ago. When I was a PC and attended road accidents." More years ago than I care to remember, he thought. The worst he had seen thirty years ago were still vivid in his imagination, despite his attempts to obliterate them. "Miss Ross, we think we may have identified the man who did this to you. If we're right, we'll have him arrested before long." He spoke more confidently than he felt. He was hoping they would be able to arrest that sadist Wally Smith before he realised they were on to him: if they had any warning, loners like him tended to disappear to another city, under another name. After two thousand years of exhortations to turn the other cheek, there was a greater demand than ever for his sort of brutality.

Zoe Ross's brain must have been working as sharply as ever, whatever her injuries and her post-traumatic shock, for she anticipated his first question. "I can't help you with any identification, you know. I never even saw him. He threw some sort of bag over my head as I got out of my car. Then he just started hitting me. I – I thought he was going to kill me."

For a moment, her lower lip quivered at the recollection, and Lambert said hastily, "Then there's no point in taking you back over it. Hopefully we'll get a confession out of the man, or find some trace of him at the scene of the crime – we had a team out there as soon as you'd been put in an ambulance to be brought here."

"Yes. I was lucky in that way, wasn't I? They said it

was a policeman who found me and called the ambulance on his mobile. How come he was there so quickly? I couldn't have lost consciousness for more than a few seconds, but he was there before I could even try to get to my feet – and was I glad to see him!"

Her brain was normal, whatever the state of her face. A sharp girl, this one. Even if unlucky in love. But he had too much experience of pretty and intelligent girls choosing awful men to be surprised by her choice of the duplicitous Ted Giles. He took a quick decision that there was no point in deceiving her about this. "The policeman was actually under orders to follow you. When you turned into the car park behind the Hare and Hounds, he waited five minutes before he followed you in. It's standard practice when people are under surveillance, to try to prevent them discovering that they're being tailed. He saw the man we think was your assailant driving away, but of course he didn't know you'd been attacked until he found you lying beside your car."

"I suppose I ought to be thankful that he was there. But why on earth was he following me?"

Lambert smiled grimly. "Because you're involved in a murder inquiry, I'm afraid. You know a man called Aubrey Bass. His van was used to dispose of the body of Ted Giles. We had him in for questioning about it. Held him for almost twenty-four hours. He claims he knows nothing about it – that his van must have been taken away without his permission. But he's a dubious ruffian, our Aubrey, and my Inspector thought it was worth keeping an eye on him when he was released.

Within an hour, you paid him a visit. Not surprisingly, he put you under surveillance after that."

"I only went there because I heard in a pub that you'd taken him into the station for questioning. I knew Aubrey Bass, just about. I knew he lived next door to Ted, because he'd ogled me once or twice when I'd been visiting. I wanted to know if Bass knew who had killed Ted – you didn't seem to be getting very far at the time. He said he knew nothing about it, but if I needed someone to take care of me, he could be the man." The mouth, which was the only recognisable part of her face, smiled wryly at the recollection. Without the accompaniment of the rest of her features, it made a bizarre effect.

"I can believe that, now. You must see that it looked pretty suspicious at the time."

"I suppose so. It looks as though I should be grateful that police help was so close at hand last night, whatever the reason."

"You shouldn't have tried to play the amateur detective. Look where it's landed you."

That miraculously untouched mouth grinned at its owner's naivety. "Are you any nearer to arresting the person who killed Ted?"

"I think we are, yes. It's a matter of putting the various pieces of the jigsaw together, and we're nearly there." Beyond her bed, he could see the formidable Sister in the doorway, looking fierce disapproval and gesturing at her watch. He said, "I'm glad that your injuries are no worse. There's one final thing. If we're right about the man who attacked you, he didn't even know you. He's a man who

203

sells his services to anyone who will pay handsomely. Can you think of anyone who might have hired him to attack you like that?"

The two dark, glistening pupils which were all he could see of her eyes fixed on his face for a moment, and he thought she was going to give him a name. Then she said softly, "No. I can't think of anyone who would want this done to me. Perhaps you'll discover that if you find the man."

He stood up, "Yes, I think we will."

But as he thanked her for her help and took his leave, he thought he already knew who had paid her attacker.

Sixteen

A ubrey Bass looked out of his window at the car park behind the block of flats. He didn't like what he saw. His van was back in its usual position, which was good. He had looked anxiously over his shoulder into its interior, the first couple of times he had used it, not liking the thought that the body of his late neighbour, Ted Giles, had been carried there on its last journey to Broughton's Ash churchyard. But he had carried a big load of lead to the scrapyard in it yesterday, and disposed of it for a good price without too many questions being asked. That made him feel that things were back to normal now, as if that more usual load had exorcised the old van of the lingering traces of a murder victim.

What Aubrey saw when he peered bleerily towards his vehicle did not please him, however. The pigs were back. He knew Sergeant "Jack" Johnson. The man had done his stint as station sergeant on the front desk of Oldford Police Station for several years, and anyone in that post had inevitably come into contact with Aubrey Bass and his life of indolence and venial crime. He was down in the car park now with another uniformed man and a couple of civilians. Aubrey, opening his window furtively and, craning his neck, could see that they were examining the ground round the rear exit from the block. They seemed to be taking measurements, as well as scanning the tarmac intently. Probably nothing to do with him, but he didn't like having the filth around the place, all the same.

He shut the window, switched on his kettle, and scratched himself comprehensively. Nosy bastards! Just as well he'd got rid of that lead yesterday.

In their different ways, three otherwise hard-headed women had behaved stupidly. And all of them for love of men who weren't worth it, thought Lambert. If it was love: for him, the difference between love and infatuation remained as difficult to define as ever, even after so many years of studying it at first hand. Passion, then. Whatever the emotion, it hadn't brought any of these three women what they desired: one of them lay in hospital and the other two were likely to end up in prison.

The dahlias which had flowered so bravely in Connie Elson's garden when Lambert and Hook had last visited the place had been cut down now by frost. They were sodden brown sticks, rearing into the air like miniature versions of the shattered trees of the Somme battlefield. Nor was the woman of the house immediately at the door to greet them, as she had been on their previous visit. The bell rang loud in the silent bungalow, and it seemed for a minute and more as if the occupant might have fled.

When she eventually opened the door, Connie Elson looked white and tense, despite the wide smile she had put on for them in the hall. This time, Lambert dispensed with the formalities of greeting. "We need to talk, Mrs

Elson," he said curtly, and walked past her without being invited into the lounge where they had sat to enjoy coffee and flapjacks on their previous visit.

She ignored his attitude, making a last attempt at conventional hospitality. "Do sit down, Superintendent. And you too – it's Sergeant Hook, isn't it?"

Lambert remained standing. "I've come here from the bedside of Miss Zoe Ross."

"That woman! I thought you'd have arrested her by now. She killed poor Ted, you know, whatever she says."

"She didn't kill Ted Giles, Mrs Elson. And now she's in hospital. I notice you don't look very surprised at that. I'm here because I think you put her there."

She abandoned her decision to sit down, drew herself instead to her full height, tried desperately to rise to this challenge she told herself she had half-expected. "Now look, Mr Lambert, you should know better than to come here making accusations like that. I haven't been out of this place in the last twenty-four hours, so—"

"I didn't say you'd attacked her yourself! Nothing so straightforward and risky as that!" Lambert, who had intended to hear her out, to let her condemn herself by over-elaboration, found himself shouting. He was suddenly weary of this woman, with her designer clothes, her expensive jewellery and her elaborate coiffure; she was at once pathetic and dangerous. Yet the brain works with amazing speed: even in his anger, he had time to wonder if he would have been so furious with the woman if her victim had been a man and not an attractive younger woman. He went on in more measured tones, "You put her in hospital as surely as if you had attacked her yourself. More surely, because the man you employed was a professional. He threw a bag over her head and beat her face without mercy; it will be a miracle if she isn't permanently scarred."

"But I didn't want—" Her hand flew to her mouth, the jewelled rings flashing as they caught the afternoon sun through the big window.

"You didn't want her hurt as badly as that? Think you can dole out violence in controlled doses, do you, like money? Well, men like Wally Smith aren't that easy to control, you see, when they have someone helpless to hit."

"You've got Wally?"

He felt a surge of triumph with that short phrase. She'd as good as admitted she'd used Smith. He might deny it all, but with her evidence they'd put him away for a long stretch. "We'll have him before the day's out. And you'll go to prison for employing him, I'm glad to say. Arrest her, Bert, and let's be out of here. We haven't any more time to waste on Mrs Elson!"

Hook pronounced the formal words of her arrest in connection with an assault on Zoe Ross. She appeared to take notice of the warning that whatever she said might later be used in evidence, for at first she said nothing. Only when she sat weeping beside Hook in the back of the car on the way to the station did she speak. Three times she said between sobs, as if it didn't just explain her conduct but excused it as well, "But I thought she'd killed Ted, you see. I knew she'd found out about Ted and me, and she must have known he was going to marry me."

She got not a word in response from either of the men in the car. As they drove into the Oldford Police Station car park, she said by way of hopeless amplification, "I thought I could frighten her into owning up!"

An hour after Connie Elson had been taken into Oldford Police Station, Colin Pitman rang his daughter from his office in Malvern. "We need to talk," he said tersely.

"Dad, we agreed we'd stay apart for a little while. Just in case they're watching us. They won't be, but just to be on the safe side."

"I know what we agreed. But I think we need to go over it all once again. I told you, they were here again on Tuesday and I had to change my story." All his life until now, he had been the strong man in her life, offering her advice and support, guiding her actions with his experience and shrewdness. Now he felt like a weak old man, pathetically dependent upon his daughter, allowing circumstances to dictate the course of his actions when he had been used to shaping them himself.

Sue Giles heard it in his voice. He would let them down, unless they bolstered him, convinced him that they had nothing to fear but their own weakness. He had phoned her before to tell her that the police had been back to talk to him on Tuesday, given her the details of the new story he had told to account for his whereabouts on that fateful Saturday night. He seemed to have forgotten all that. He needed the physical support of a meeting with her, the reassurance of her calm presence at his side. In all truth, she didn't feel as cool and confident as she was trying to sound for her father, but she mustn't let him know that. "All right, Dad. Come over here by all means, if you think it will help. Make it in about an hour. Graham's coming round after school. We'll have a council of war." She gave an involuntary nervous laugh at the phrase as she put down the phone.

Sergeant 'Jack' Johnson had new men in his team. He was instructing them in the painstaking, boring and just occasionally rewarding techniques they had to employ. They'd already covered the area round where Aubrey Bass's van was parked four days earlier, with little added to what they already new. It was important that now that they were back to stake out the area around the exit, there was full attention to the task, with no weary sense of déjà vu.

Crawling around wet tarmac on a bleak November day with tweezers and a small stainless-steel dish for your findings was not a pleasant task, though at least the signing cards of dogs or cats were not evident on this particular patch. He told one new man how even a dog turd had become vital evidence on one memorable occasion in the early nineties: they had parcelled the distinctive excreta carefully into a plastic bag and some forensic genius had later been able to place a particular dog (and thus a particular owner) in a specific spot on a certain day.

The young man did not seem very impressed with this particular example of the rewards of diligence. But the message about detail obviously went home, for ten minutes later he brought his Sergeant a dish full of the tiny detritus that would only have been visible to a man on hands and knees in that draughty expanse. Though he did not say so, Johnson could see at a glance that most of the items were likely to be unhelpful in establishing the particular spot where Ted Giles had met his end. The tiny shards of broken glass did not connect with the method by which Giles had been killed. The rusting pin looked to his experienced eye as if it had lain here for far longer than eleven days.

One item, however, Sergeant Johnson thought very interesting. He always told his team to keep an open mind about what might be useful to forensic: they were to collect anything and everything, leaving it to the boffins to pick out what was relevant to a particular investigation. But whenever it was possible, he examined the clothing, and especially the outer clothing, worn by murder victims before his SOC investigations, so that he might instantly recognise anything at a scene of crime which might be significant. And on this occasion, he found much to interest him in a tiny cluster of near-black fibres which his acolyte's tweezers had retrieved.

Ted Giles had been wearing a navy-blue V-neck sweater of pure wool when his body had been found. The Constable was able to tell Johnson exactly where he had found the fibres, ground into the rough surface of the tarmac. Very much as though a man had been flung on his back here as he fell with a wire drawn fatally tight around his neck. But that was for other, more scientific minds and their technology to decide. Sergeant Johnson measured the exact distance from the double doors of the flats and marked it carefully on the neat scale plan he had drawn of the area.

He saw the caretaker, watching their activities curiously from the hall of the flats as he pretended to sweep the tiled floor. "I wanted a quick word," Johnson said. "This area hasn't been swept since the night of the tenth of November, has it?"

The man was around sixty, with thick glasses and a droopy moustache. He was immediately defensive. "Not my responsibility, that. There's a contract with a gardening firm for all outside maintenance. I pick up any bits of litter I see, keep the place tidy, like, but that's all."

"Good. I'm only anxious to check that things haven't been disturbed here since the death of Mr Giles. The outside maintenance firm hasn't been here since then?"

"No. We don't see much of them once the winter comes and the grass stops growing."

The man was prepared to enlarge upon the deficiencies of the absent contractors, but Johnson said, "You've recently replaced the bulb in this outside light, haven't you?"

The caretaker looked at him suspiciously over his moustache. "Yes. How do you know that?"

"Superintendent Lambert of Oldford CID told me. You were putting a new bulb in when he came here to look at Mr Giles's flat on Tuesday of last week."

The caretaker seemed impressed by this precision. "That's right. I was up me ladder when he and that Sergeant came. They asked me for directions to Mr Giles's flat."

"Do you happen to know when the old bulb failed? Was the light off over the previous weekend?"

The man was defensive again. "I couldn't say for certain. I replaced it as soon as I was told about it. I'm not here weekends, you see. I don't live on the premises. I only do mornings." He leaned forward a little to impart a confidence. "I'm more your part-time odd-job man, really. Cleaning of the halls and landings and minor repairs. They called it internal maintenance, at first. Then they thought it might make the place a bit more secure if people thought the block had a caretaker, so they called me that."

That explained his presence here: Johnson hadn't thought these flats grand or numerous enough to warrant the high maintenance charges of a resident caretaker. He said, "So it's quite likely that this light was off on that Saturday night when Mr Giles died?"

"Probably was. According to Mrs Clarkson who reported it, it had been off for the whole of the weekend." The caretaker leaned forward again, his sense of his own importance growing as he realised he might be assisting with a murder inquiry. "As a matter of fact, the bulb hadn't just failed. It had been removed. Never happened before, that hasn't."

Sergeant Johnson rounded up his SOC team and took his findings back to CID. He carried the sealed plastic envelope with the navy fibres in it as carefully as if it were the crown jewels. And he had no doubt that Superintendent Lambert would be very interested to know about that missing bulb.

Sue Giles's house looked as incongruously large and grand for a single occupant as it had on their first visit a week ago. Six bedrooms at least: this place should have had children in it, thought Bert Hook, contrasting it with his own modern semi, increasingly cramped as his two boys grew towards adolescence. But it was as well that the ill-starred Giles union had spawned no children.

The gardener was wheeling his cycle away from the big garden shed as they parked in front of the house in the November twilight. He looked at them curiously, then switched his lamps on and pedalled slowly away. The long neat beds had been cleared now of the last of the autumn's flowers; there was not a leaf to be seen on the large areas of trimly edged green lawn. The lights were switched on in the hall and several rooms of the big modern house, making the day seem already darker than it was. Hook's watch showed twenty-five past four.

Sue Giles opened the oak front door herself. "Superintendent Lambert. And Sergeant Hook. It isn't convenient to see you just now, I'm afraid. Mr Reynolds is here, you see. And my father, whom I know you've met. It's Dad's birthday, you see, and—"

"On the contrary, that will be most convenient for our purposes. Since all three of you are involved in this."

She stood her ground in the doorway for a moment, blocking his entry. Because of the step, she stared straight into his hard grey eyes from no more than two feet. Then she moved aside and allowed the two big men to pass her before she slowly shut the door.

In the elegant drawing room, where Sue Giles had talked to them a week earlier about her relationship with her murdered husband, Colin Pitman and Graham Reynolds sat in armchairs on opposite sides of the fireplace. Pitman was on the edge of his and Reynolds was leaning forward, as though the haulage proprietor and the man who planned to become his son-in-law had been in

214

animated conversation before this unwelcome interruption.

Sue Giles made a brave show at relaxation in the face of this intrusion. "Mr Lambert and his Sergeant have something that apparently can't wait. Perhaps we can deal with it quickly and carry on with your birthday, Dad."

If it was meant to convey a message to her father, it had the opposite effect from that she intended. A look of puzzlement passed across the broad face of Colin Pitman. Obviously the excuse of a birthday celebration was news to him. A long second passed before he said, "Yes. It really isn't very convenient that you should come here now, Superintendent. But if you must interrupt us, please don't take any longer than is necessary."

He was trying to be masterful, as he was used to being in his business. It was curious how words lacked all conviction when the speaker couldn't muster the right tone, thought Hook.

Lambert, deciding that a man who was normally direct and honest would be most easily discomfited when his lies were exposed, said, "I shan't apologise. That would be absurd, when we have come here to arrest you."

Sue Giles was the first to recover. "That's ridiculous talk. After my father's done his very best to cooperate with you, it's—"

"On the contrary, he's fed us a string of lies to try to conceal his true whereabouts on the night of your husband's murder." Lambert had ignored the woman, never taking his eyes from Pitman's too-revealing face. "He told us he was at home on that night. When that was exposed as a lie, he tried to spin us an absurd story about spending the evening in Birmingham with a prostitute."

Pitman found his tongue at last, knowing he couldn't let his daughter go on defending him. "I was with a tart, Lambert. I told you, I drove round for an hour before I nerved myself to approach her. I'm not proud of it. Why you should come throwing it into my face in front of my daughter I don't know, but you'd better have good reason." His voice was low, gravelly, like that of a mortally sick man.

"You didn't drive anywhere, Mr Pitman. Your Jaguar was sitting in your garage when our burglar broke into it. He assured me of that this morning."

Lambert was almost sorry for this big man who had floundered so far out of his depth. He had subsided into the big chair, a wounded bear who needed to be put out of his misery. He didn't even try the lame excuse of a hire car. He said dully, repeating a formula which had lost its validity even for him, "I was in Birmingham with a tart. You'll have to find her."

Lambert said shortly, "You were in Killarney with your daughter. Pretending to be this man."

Graham Reynolds said, "I don't know where you get your information from, Superintendent, but you'd better change your sources. I was at the Lakeside Hotel with Sue on that night. Surely you've checked that out." He moved across to her, put his arm through hers, as though both of them might gather strength from the contact.

"Of course we have. We found adjoining rooms were booked in the names of Mrs Giles and Mr Reynolds. Unusually squeamish, that."

"That's our business!" Sue Giles's voice was clear, but taut with tension. "If you're going to say I wasn't in Killarney on the night when Ted died, then you're—"

"Oh, you were there all right. But the man in the adjoining room was your father, not Graham Reynolds."

"Look, if you're going to make wild accusations like that, you'd better—"

"We have a detailed description of the man who was with you from the Irish Gardi. If it should be necessary, the man with you will be formally identified in due course."

In the pause which followed Lambert's calm statement, Sue Giles drew in a long breath, mustering further defiance. But before she could utter it, her father, sitting still as a carved image in his armchair, said dully, "Leave it, Sue, it's over. All right, Superintendent, I was the man in Killarney with my daughter that weekend. That's why I had to tell you such tales. I didn't enjoy doing that. And I didn't know Graham was going to kill Giles. And neither did Sue. She—"

"Shut up, Dad! For Christ's sake, shut up! Graham didn't kill Ted. It's a ridiculous idea!" She was very shrill now, looking to the man who stood beside her to come in and support her. But Graham Reynolds looked briefly from her to Pitman without a word; then his wide eyes were drawn back to Lambert's, like a rabbit hypnotised by the stoat which will finish its life. He said nothing.

Lambert looked back at him steadily. "It was only today that we established where the killing took place. We know now that the bulb was removed from the outside light over the exit from the flats where Giles lived. He was due to meet Miss Zoe Ross on that

217

Saturday night. You waited outside the flats until he came out to the car park, then killed him from behind by garrotting him with a piece of wire."

Sue Giles sank down on to a chair, her hand still clinging awkwardly to its contact with her lover as she subsided, until it fell limply to her side. She said, in a voice they could only just catch, "Tell him you didn't do it, Graham."

Reynolds remained standing. He said bleakly, "What's the use? They have everything they want." His previously impassive face broke suddenly into an awful, mirthless smile. "Just as that sod Giles had everything I wanted. He made me look a fool in the school, you know. Made me look small in front of the children." For a moment, his bitterness made it seem as if he thought that alone was reason enough to kill a man.

Lambert said quietly, "I expect Giles also threatened to expose your gambling debts to the powers that be."

"Of course he did. When I pressed him to get on with the divorce, he threatened me with that. Said he had religious scruples about divorce because he was brought up as a Catholic. His Church didn't allow divorce, he said. He laughed about that, said how convenient it was. When I said the law wouldn't allow him to hold things up indefinitely, he said he'd take Sue for everything he could, that there wouldn't be much left for me when he'd finished. It was my idea that Sue and her dad would establish an alibi for me, whilst I – whilst I dealt with Giles. They're not guilty. They didn't know I was going to kill him."

A court would need some convincing of that, thought Lambert sourly. He said, "You planned this killing very carefully." With malice aforethought, in the proper legal phrase, but he wouldn't risk stopping Reynolds from talking by using it here.

In the way of men who have lost all moral balance, Reynolds seemed for a moment to think he was being flattered. "Yes, I suppose I did. I didn't want my own car to be seen anywhere in the vicinity, but I had a key which would open that scruffy bugger Bass's old van. I'd tried it a few nights earlier – lots of keys will fit older Fords, you know, but they've tightened up now." He had almost brightened with this illustration of his ingenuity. "I knew he was going out to see Zoe Ross that Saturday night – he'd taunted me with this younger woman when I'd tried to talk to him about Sue's divorce earlier in the day. I removed the bulb by the back exit from the flats and just waited for him in the dark with my piano wire. It was easy."

"Then you left his body face down in Bass's van for a couple of hours." The hypostasis on the front of the corpse was one of the first facts they had been given by forensic.

Reynolds wasn't surprised by their knowledge: he looked as if he expected them now to know every detail. He said, as if still demonstrating his own thoughtfulness in the matter, "I thought at first of dumping him in the Severn. But the roads were quite busy at that time on Saturday night – it couldn't have been later than half-past eight when I killed him. I drove around for a while, then went into a country pub and had a drink – I left him under an old curtain in the back of the van, but I locked it carefully."

He looked around the circle of people with an awful smile at this recollection, but did not register the horror-stricken faces of Pitman and his daughter, nor the quiet, attentive eyes of the policemen. "I waited until after closing time, then drove to Broughton's Ash and tipped him over the wall into the churchyard. It must have been around midnight when I got back and put Bass's van back in the car park of the flats. I walked home from there. I don't think that dozy sod Bass even realised his van had been taken and returned."

He looked for a moment as if he expected to be congratulated on his planning and execution of the crime. Then the silence stretched and his face slowly darkened as the enormity of his situation finally sank in. Hook pronounced the words of arrest on the three of them whilst his chief used his radio to call up the car they had left in the road outside.

Sue Giles and Graham Reynolds were handcuffed and led to that car by three burly policemen. Pitman sat with Lambert in the back of the other car while Hook drove. The big man stared unbelievingly back at the house he had bought for his daughter and her ill-fated husband, then at the familiar countryside he had grown to love as he built his business.

There was no word spoken, but, as sometimes happens when the game is over between criminal and detective, between hunted and hunter, there was a kind of kinship between the two big men in the back of the car. The detective who knew now that the wife he relied upon was coming back to him from hospital and the man who had made himself an accessory to murder because he had so lacked the guidance of the wife he had lost.